THE CHASTE LEGACY

by

SUSANNA HUGHES

Published by **CHIMERA**
ISBN 9781780804569

Chapter One

Corinda Chaste lay naked on the large double bed. The windows, with their bleached wooden shutters, were open and she could hear the sound of the waves breaking on the beach. The scent of jasmine and bougainvillaea wafted in on the light breeze that rustled the thin white muslin curtains. Her young body tingled, anticipating the pleasure to come. She could see Arabella through the open bathroom door as she stood in the shower, and felt a surge of desire as she watched the water cascading over the ripe curves of her body. Arabella was a brunette with short hair and large dark brown eyes, and though she was older than Corinda by some twenty years would have had no trouble passing for her sister. In terms of the smoothness of her complexion, the suppleness of her limbs and the youthful sparkle in her eyes, Arabella was Corinda's equal.

Corinda watched as Arabella's hands soaped her firm round breasts, her slightly plump belly and the thick, black hair of her pubes; she lathered them until they were coated in white foam then allowed the shower to wash it all away. She soaped her plum-shaped bottom. Her buttocks were pliant and generously fleshed. She rubbed between her legs, then turned into the flow of water until all the white lather was washed away.

The sight made Corinda's sex moisten. She ran her hand down the soft blonde hair at the base of her belly and quickly parted the thin lips of her sex, eager to find her clitoris. Involuntarily she let out a breathy exclamation as the little nut of nerves responded to this first assault with a spasm of pleasure. Snapping her legs together, she trapped her finger between her thighs and squeezed it hard, producing another wave of pleasure as it pressed tightly against her sex.

'Are you starting without me?' Arabella said walking up to the side of the bed. She dried her body lazily with a towel as water dripped on the blue tiled floor.

'I was watching you,' Corinda said by way of explanation.

'Watching me shower?'

'Yes. You know I love your body.'

'And it loves you.'

Arabella threw the towel aside. Though it was late afternoon, and the Greek sun had begun to set, the room was warm and most of the moisture on her body had already evaporated. She watched as Corinda opened her legs wide, and moved her fingers down between her labia to spread them open so Arabella would be able to see the wetness of her vagina. It was scarlet and glistening.

Corinda was simply beautiful. She had long strawberry-blonde hair, lightened by exposure to the almost constant sun on the island. Her body was bronzed for the same reason, the absence of bikini marks testifying to the fact that the girl spent most of her time outdoors quite naked. She was tall and slender with long legs, sculpted by constant exercise into supple contours, and a narrow waist. Her breasts were full and pendulous. In contrast her belly was completely flat, a plateau marked on each side by the distinct ridges of her hipbones.

Corinda's face was peerless. She had high and hollow cheekbones, a thin straight nose, and a perfectly symmetrical mouth with lips that had a waxy smoothness. Her large blue eyes expressed an innocent eagerness to experience all the joys of life. But there was a toughness too, suggesting she would be able to cope with its disappointments.

'Aren't you going to lie down?' Corinda said, pouting slightly. She pushed one finger into her vagina, feeling the silky wet flesh close around it as though it were trying to suck it in.

'It's your birthday tomorrow,' Arabella said.

'I know. I'm eighteen. Don't keep me waiting Bella; I'm so horny.'

'You must not say such things. I thought I'd brought you up to know better.'

'But it's true. Can't you see for yourself?'

'I've got a present for you.'

'The only present I want is you,' Corinda said, wriggling her finger deeper into her sex.

'It's a way of giving you more pleasure, Corinda.'

'More pleasure?' Corinda looked puzzled.

Arabella opened the top drawer of the bedside table and extracted a rectangular box wrapped in bright blue paper. She placed it on the bed. Over the last year Arabella had taught Corinda every pleasure that two women could give to each other; every pleasure, that is, bar one. She had saved this until last; saved it deliberately for the eve of her eighteenth birthday.

'Aren't you going to open it?'

Corinda sat up, abandoning her sex with a certain reluctance. She picked the box up and tore the wrapping paper away impatiently. Inside she found a wooden box with a hinged lid. There was a little brass catch on one side, which she opened, swinging the lid up. The interior of the box was lined with red velvet.

Lying in the padding that was moulded to fit around it snugly, was a long cylindrical object with a bulbous base, made from cream-coloured plastic. It was a perfect replica of an erect male penis, complete in every detail, from the ridges at the bottom of the glans to the large scrotum.

'You know what it is?' Arabella asked, as Corinda pulled it from the box.

'Yes, I think so.' Unaccountably, Corinda felt her sex throbbing as she allowed her fingers to caress the phallus. 'This is what a man looks like, isn't it?'

'Exactly.'

Corinda had never seen a man, at least not close up, and certainly never naked and erect. This was the Chaste legacy. Twelve years ago on the death of her father, his will had dictated that she be brought to the island and educated there specifically by women. She was to be allowed no contact with men. Arabella, one of the two trustees of the will, had fulfilled its provisions to the letter.

But tomorrow all that would change. Tomorrow Corinda came of age and could no longer be governed by the provisions of the will. She would be able to choose for herself what life she led. As much as Arabella would have liked to keep her on the island, as much as she wished to husband her body for herself, she knew she could not. She had to let the girl go her own way. She had made arrangements accordingly. She would encounter men in the real world and Arabella wanted her to know what was in store, if only in the most rudimentary of ways.

'And this goes inside me?' Like every other aspect of her education, biology had not been neglected.

'Yes.'

'Oh, Arabella, can I try? It's made me feel so wet already.' Corinda could feel a little river of juice trickling out of her vagina and on to her thigh.

'Good. You have to be wet. That's it.'

Arabella sat on the edge of the bed. She took Corinda's cheek in her hand, and kissed her softly on the lips before pushing her back on to the bed. She took the dildo from Corinda's hand.

Corinda's pulse was racing as she felt Arabella trail the tip of the phallus down over her belly. She opened her legs wide, ready to receive it. Though she had never admitted it to Arabella, she had often used objects to penetrate her sex - the handle of her hairbrush was her favourite - when she masturbated; more recently she had being doing this with increased frequency. Though she had never seen a man close up, she had glimpsed them over the fences of the estate and had often imagined what it would be like to convert the cold, clinical language of the biology textbooks into hot, passionate practice. She had not told Arabella about that either.

Arabella nudged the dildo between Corinda's labia.

'It feels so hard,' Corinda said, wriggling herself on it, impatient for the feeling of penetration.

But Arabella resisted the temptation to plunge it straight into Corinda's vagina. Instead she used the tip to circle her clitoris, as she had done so many times before with her tongue or her finger.

'Please...' Corinda begged softly.

Arabella knelt up on the bed beside the blonde. 'You want it?'

'Oh, yes.'

Corinda felt the dildo ploughing the furrow of her labia until it reached the gate of her vagina. Her whole body seemed to be pulsing and it felt as though her heart was in her mouth. Nothing she had used before was as big as this, or as authentic. She had lost her hymen when she had been riding a horse over a particularly high jump, so she knew - as did Arabella - that there was no barrier to the dildo's progress and there would be no pain.

Arabella eased the dildo up into the mouth of Corinda's vagina; it was so large her labia was stretched taut by it. She pushed it forward until the ridge at the bottom of the carefully sculpted glans had disappeared.

'Higher,' Corinda urged.

'Are you sure?'

'Yes, push it further.'

Arabella pushed it deeper, watching the cream plastic disappear. She heard

4

Corinda gasp but just as she was about to withdraw it for fear of hurting her, Corinda reached down, grabbed her wrist, and forced her to thrust the dildo as deep as it would go.

'Yes,' she said triumphantly, as she felt her sex contract around the invader. The dildo provoked a flood of feelings so intense her body arched up off the bed, every sinew and nerve singing with pleasure. Before, when only fingers had worked on her sex, her orgasm would build slowly. But with this hard phallus buried inside her she reacted instantaneously. She felt a crescendo of intense pleasure breaking over the head of the dildo and rushing through her body. It was amplified by the thoughts flashing through her head. This was what a man would feel like; this big, this broad. It was like taking a man for the first time.

Arabella watched calmly. She saw the crisis pass and Corinda's body sink back onto the bed. But she held the dildo in place, knowing the first orgasm would leave the young girl breathless for more. At the same time she reached forward and kissed her.

The feeling of Arabella's soft, fleshy lips and her hot tongue plunging into her mouth, produced another tremor of exquisite sensation in Corinda's body.

'Is this what it's like? Is this what a man is like?' Corinda writhed down on the phallus.

To be honest, Arabella didn't know. Her sexual experience was limited to women. But she used her imagination. 'Yes, a little. They are hard like this, and thrusting. The pleasure between two women is different, but you must know what it's like to take a man inside you. That is what they'll want.'

'But they will be hot with semen. They ejaculate, don't they?' Corinda remembered that word from the textbooks. 'Oh, Bella, give me more.'

Arabella leant forward. She kissed Corinda's neck, working her mouth down the corded sinews to the hollow of the collarbone, then on to her breasts. She sucked at each nipple in turn, then used her teeth to pinch them lightly. She feasted on the firm but supple flesh, moulding it with her free hand, squeezing and kneading each breast in turn. Slowly her mouth sank lower, to Corinda's flat stomach. The tip of her tongue plunged into Corinda's deep navel.

'What are you going to do?' Corinda said, her voice trembling with the feelings Arabella was inducing. Her sex was contracting against the dildo as though trying to milk it.

'Hush,' whispered Arabella.

'It feels so heavenly.'

Arabella's tongue lapped at the base of Corinda's stomach. She allowed the dildo to move down, slippery with the juices that had anointed it so comprehensively, then pushed it back up again, until the imitation scrotum was hard against Corinda's labia, the lips stretched taut by its girth.

'Oh, that's so good,' the blonde said, wriggling down on the phallus.

Arabella's tongue lapped over the soft pubic hair, then eased into the crease of Corinda's sex, finding her clitoris immediately. The little promontory had swollen out from beneath the hood of flesh that normally protected it. Arabella tapped it with the tip of her tongue and felt Corinda's body tense.

'Oh that's - that's...' Corinda couldn't believe the feeling. Arabella had used her tongue on her a hundred times, but now the pleasure she felt instantly merged with the new sensations the dildo was generating deep inside her. Once again her whole body shook; every nerve, it seemed, thrilled to the overall sensation.

But Arabella had no intention of leaving it there. Grasping the base of the dildo she eased it out slightly then pushed it back, establishing a rhythm. Using exactly the same tempo she pushed Corinda's clitoris from side to side with the tip of her tongue. Slowly she increased the stroke of the dildo, bringing it out further so it would have further to go back in.

'Oh, Bella, Bella,' Corinda cried. The rhythm was perfect, the sensations already surpassing her first orgasm. She knew this was how a cock would feel. She knew this was what a man would do to her. She could imagine what it would be like; how his weight would crush down on her and his buttocks would rise and fall as he drove his erection into her body. She had seen a young boy over the fence, working in the vineyards on the other side. He had been stripped to the waist and his muscular body rippled as he sawed at the vines, pruning the old wood. Corinda imagined him, his mouth kissing her, his chest crushing her breasts, his strong fingers touching her, his cock buried where the dildo was now. She was coming. Every muscle in her body was knitted into a rigid contour; her back arched off the bed like a long bow. As she felt Arabella's tongue drag across her clitoris and the dildo buried itself in her sex again her orgasm exploded, releasing a torrent of energy that sucked her into a maelstrom of pleasure.

Arabella lifted her head and took her hand from the base of the dildo. She watched as Corinda's body sank back on to the bed, the rigidity leaving her limbs. Corinda flinched reflexively as the dildo slid out of her sex.

'Happy birthday,' Arabella said softly.

'It's a wonderful present.'

'Did it feel good?'

'Oh yes.' She didn't tell Arabella what had been going on in her mind. 'Why haven't we used it before?'

Arabella had used a dildo frequently and enjoyed the pleasure it gave her, though she never thought of it as a substitute for a man. Conversely she had held it back from Corinda, until now, because it represented the masculinity her father had been trying to protect her from. 'It wasn't the right time.'

'Can I use it on you now?' Corinda asked enthusiastically. She was keen to give her tutor equal pleasure.

'Yes, if that's what you want.'

Corinda sat up. As she kissed Arabella she could taste her own juices on Arabella's lips, as she had done many times before. Gently she pushed her back on to the bed and knelt beside her.

Leaning forward she cradled Arabella's left breast in both hands and sucked on its cherry-sized nipple. She repeated the process with the right breast, then groped around with her hand until it lighted upon the bulbous base of the dildo. It was sticky and wet. She suddenly imagined what it would be like to wrap her hand around a real live cock, hot and pulsing at her touch.

Feeling her heart beat faster again she brought the dildo up to Arabella's belly, and nosed it down into her thick black pubic hair. As it descended Arabella opened her legs and bent them at the knee.

'I'm very wet, Corinda. Doing that to you has made me very excited,' Arabella said.

'And me.'

Corinda worked the glans-shaped tip down between Arabella's legs. She could see the clitoris, as the dildo stretched the labia apart, so it was not difficult to nose the phallus up again and centre it perfectly on the little knot of flesh.

'Yes,' Arabella said. She had raised her head to watch what Corinda was doing, but allowed it to fall back as a wave of pleasure coursed out from her clit.

Corinda pushed the dildo up and down and saw Arabella's body tense. With the fingers of her other hand she stroked the tops of her thighs, then angled them inward until she could feel the opening of her vagina. Immediately she thrust two, then three fingers deep inside her, as deep as they would go. She had done this many times but the feeling of Arabella's silky tight sex always thrilled her. Her own body pulsed at the sensation; her clitoris, trapped between her thighs, throbbed with the memory of the passion she had experienced only minutes before.

Taking her fingers out she replaced them with the dildo, driving it as high as it would go, the penetration made effortless by Arabella's copious fluids. Learning her lesson quickly, as all Corinda's tutors had said she was able to do, she dipped her head forward and flicked out her tongue to press against Arabella's clitoris. Then, just as Arabella had done to her, she drew the phallus in and out of her vagina, as her tongue agitated the engorged clitoris from side to side. Instantly she felt Arabella's body tense.

For a moment Arabella raised her head and looked down her body to watch Corinda. The girl's long blonde hair was sweeping over her navel as she moved her head; her breasts squashed against her thighs as she crouched forward. Then the sensation her body was generating became too self-absorbing and she had to drop her head back and close her eyes, luxuriating in the sheer exhilaration of what was being done to her. Immediately an orgasm seized her, provoked by the head of the dildo and the delicate movements of Corinda's tongue. She clutched at the sheet, needing something to hold on to as she plunged over a cliff of pleasure, and fell deeper and deeper into an abyss of bottomless joy.

Slowly she clawed her way back up to the real world. She raised herself on her elbows and looked down at Corinda. 'Come here, my sweet thing. Let's be together now.'

The dildo was a new toy but the older, more established rituals asserted themselves again. Corinda knew at once what Arabella wanted. Moving towards her head she swung a thigh over the older woman's shoulder and planted her sex firmly on her mouth. Then she centred her own lips on the woman's sex.

Thus they were joined, as they had been joined before, their actions and reactions synchronised, their bodies feeling the same thing and doing the same thing; each touch, each lick, each kiss they gave exactly the same as they received.

What had gone before was a prelude to this. Though both had experienced shattering orgasms as the dildo had invaded them, it was this familiar combination that would deliver to them the most exquisite pleasure of all. Corinda felt Arabella's tongue lapping at her sex, as though she were licking an ice cream, and responded at once by doing the same to Arabella. The dildo had slipped from her body and Corinda replaced it with her fingers, this time sliding another finger alongside them into the woman's anus. She knew Arabella would do the same to her, and sure enough felt fingers penetrate her front and rear.

They rolled and rocked on the bed, hugging together, their breasts crushed, their nipples as hard as pebbles. They were so close in every way, they could feel exactly what the other felt. In fact it was almost impossible to distinguish who was feeling what. Their bodies trembled with pleasure; the sharp, rapid orgasms they had experienced with the dildo were replaced by a long slow build up, a gathering tidal wave of passion that swept over everything in its path.

As Corinda felt the wave mounting higher in her own body the effect was doubled because she could feel it in Arabella too. Eventually, after what might have been seconds but felt like hours, the wave reached a peak with the sensations so intense neither could stand it any longer. There it stayed, seemingly suspended in mid-air, a wall of trembling water waiting to crash down. When it did both females underwent the same catharsis at the same time, both clinging to each other for support, arms wrapped around each other's thighs, mouths pressed to each other's sex-lips, as though afraid they would be washed away by the surging tide of exhilaration.

How many times had Corinda come like this, joined to Arabella, their bodies intertwined to form some strange two-headed beast? It was what Arabella had taught her, and she was grateful for it. But tonight her climax had been different. Tonight, deep in her sex, the dildo had left an impression, like a key pressed into soap. Tonight, though it was Arabella's artful tongue and fingers that had brought her off, it was the feeling of the dildo that had been the most powerful provocation. It had left her with a burning desire to experience the real thing.

Disentangled from each other, Arabella picked the dildo up from the bed, dried it with a towel and replaced it in the padded box. 'Let's go down to the beach for a walk,' she said. 'There are things I have to tell you, Corinda. The time has come.'

The giant orange ball of the sun had almost sunk below the horizon, colouring the whole sky with shades of burnt sienna. It gave the calm sea the appearance of liquid gold. The only sound was the gentle lapping of the tiny waves at the water's edge; a regular soothing sound that seemed to match the beat of Corinda's heart.

They sat side by side on the soft white sand, both wearing brightly coloured silk wraps tied loosely around the bodies which were still prone to little tremors and thrills of pleasure from their lovemaking.

'You understand why you're here, don't you?' Arabella said.

'Here on the island?' Corinda was digging her foot into the sand, making little patterns with her toes.

'Yes.'

'It's what my father wanted. It was in his will, his legacy to me.'

'Exactly. Just after you were born your mother had - well, let's say it was an accident. It was caused by two rather nasty men. And your father was very bitter about it. He loved your mother very much, Corinda, and he just couldn't stop thinking about what had happened to her. I think it drove him a little bit mad. He didn't want the same thing to happen to you. So, a couple of years later when he found out he was dying - well, he made this will...'

'For me to come here?'

'I've done everything he asked of me, Corinda. No man has ever been allowed into the estate.' Arabella paused, looking into Corinda's big blue eyes.

'But?' Corinda asked expectantly.

'Tomorrow you come of age, legally speaking. You can no longer be bound by the terms of the will. It is up to you to choose what you do. I think he hoped you would want to stay here, that you would love it so much you would never want to be part of the real world. But I know that is not true, is it, Corinda?'

'The real world? You mean England.'

'England first.'

'You're sending me to England!' Corinda jumped up on her knees and faced Arabella.

'It's your choice, of course, but I've arranged for you to go to university. There were two trustees of your father's will; myself and Andrew Morrison. Andrew was your father's solicitor but unfortunately he died last year. His son has taken over. He agrees with what I propose wholeheartedly. Tomorrow he's arriving on your father's old yacht. He will sail you back to England.'

'Really? Really? I can't believe it.'

'Is that what you want, Corinda?'

'Oh yes, yes. It's brilliant. It's great. I can't believe it. I mean I love it here, but there's so much else to see in the world. I can't imagine what it will be like. I've read so much about it. All the people and traffic and shops...' She was going to add *men* but thought better of it. Suddenly another thought struck her. 'But what about you?'

'I shall stay here. Under the terms of the will, if I carried out all my duties the house becomes mine.'

'So I can come back whenever I want?'

'Of course you can. This will always be your home.'

'What's he like, Bella?'

'Who?'

'The other trustee.'

'Tim Morrison. Well, I've never met him. We've talked on the phone. He seems very business-like. We've arranged for you to stay in your father's house in London. There's a trust to provide you with all the income you need. Then you can decide what subject you want to read at university.'

'Oh Bella, I can't believe it. When will he be here?'

'I had a message from him by radio. The yacht should arrive tomorrow evening.'

'When we're having the party?'

'Yes, he'll probably in time for that.'

Corinda's excitement was doused by a wave of sadness. She had been happy on the island despite the strange circumstances. And she loved Arabella more than she thought she would love anyone in the world. It was going to be difficult to leave her.

'I'll miss you, Bella.'

'No you won't; you'll be much too excited to miss me.'

'That's not true.'

'I'll always be here for you.' Arabella stroked Corinda's cheek, wondering if she would ever want to come back once she had discovered the lure of the big city and, more importantly, the advantages of the opposite sex. Given the exigencies of the Chaste legacy, she hoped she had done everything she could to make the girl's life a happy one. Perhaps she should not have introduced her to the pleasures of the flesh, but that was part of the real world too. She had always known Corinda would want to leave the island but to let her go without at least some knowledge of sex would have been negligent; that was how she justified it to herself in the watches of the night.

They held the party on the beach. Chinese lanterns on tall cane poles had been dug into the sand in a semicircle, and a barbecue provided Greek specialities: marinated lamb, quails roasted on a spit, and local giant prawns split open and grilled with garlic. The local wine flowed, served from large pottery jugs, and a small band played the infectious rhythms of Greek music. The band, like all the guests, were women. All Corinda's tutors from past and present had been invited, and some had been ferried in specially from the mainland. Women had been employed to teach her to ride, to swim, to play tennis and water-ski, as well as to educate her in more formal disciplines. Corinda was glad to see them again.

But whoever she found herself talking to, it was hard not to glance up at the sleek white yacht that had dropped anchor just beyond the outcrop of rocks that created a natural bay in front of the private beach. She was anxious to catch her first glimpse of Tim Morrison.

The yacht was festooned with lights, like a giant Christmas tree bobbing on the sea. In fact Corinda did not see the young solicitor walk down the gangplank, hanging diagonally from the side of the boat, and get into the sleek speedboat that would bring him to the island. The first she was aware of it was the noise of the engines approaching.

There was a small jetty where most of the supplies for the house were landed and Corinda could see Arabella waiting at the end of it. She saw her help a man ashore but it was too dark to see what he looked like.

Excusing herself from the conversation she was having with the woman who had taught her maths, Corinda ran across the beach, her heart in her mouth. As the beach dipped down towards the sea she lost sight of the jetty behind a bank of palm trees, and by the time she had climbed the stone steps that led up to it, Arabella and the man had gone.

Calming herself, and trying to tell herself to behave less like a lovesick schoolgirl now that she was eighteen, she took the long path that led from the jetty into the house. Her excitement at the prospect of meeting a man face to face for the first time in adulthood was increased by curiosity. She had read about men and knew they were fundamentally different to women, not just biologically but in a hundred other ways. There was even, some writers said, a chemical reaction between a man and a woman. The young man she had seen in the vineyard, who had become the subject of her sexual fantasies, had been too far away to test the accuracy of that theory. She was bursting to know what it would be like to see a man close up, to touch his hand and feel his flesh.

She walked into the house and through to the sitting room where she could see Arabella pouring champagne into two tall glasses. And there he was, standing with his back to her in a white linen suit.

'Corinda,' Arabella said, handing the man a glass, 'this is Tim Morrison.'

He turned and smiled, extending his hand to her. 'Very pleased to meet you, Ms Chaste.'

He was handsome. He wasn't Heathcliff or Mr Darcy, or any of the other classical romantic heroes Corinda had read about in her English literature course, but there was no question that he was an attractive man. He was younger than she had imagined and very tall, with thick blond hair and pale blue eyes. His face was open with a rather small, delicate nose, a square chin and a fleshy mouth. He had the sort of smile that was instantly infectious, making everyone around him smile too.

'Did you have a good journey?' Corinda asked as she shook his hand. Her fingers seemed to tingle as he touched them.

'Wonderful. Beautiful weather. This is my holiday really. I'm combining a little bit of business with a lot of pleasure.'

'You like sailing?' Arabella asked.

'No, not at all, but that boat isn't like sailing. It's like a floating hotel. It's amazing.'

His eyes were looking at Corinda in a way that made her feel distinctly uncomfortable. She was wearing a thin silk dress patterned with enormous sunflowers, and as her nipples puckered she was glad she had decided to wear a bra.

'It's so nice to meet you after all this time,' he continued. 'I mean over the years I've heard so much about you, from my father.'

Corinda was examining him minutely. She was fascinated by his chin, and the comparative roughness of his skin where he had shaved. She had an overwhelming desire to embrace him, to see what his body would feel like. She thought it would be hard and strong, not like the softness she felt with Arabella. The thought of it made her feel hot inside.

'Well, come and join the party,' Arabella said. 'Corinda is all packed. We'll have her cases sent over to the yacht tonight, then you can make an earlier start in the morning.'

'That would be best,' he said.

'How long will it take to get to England?' Corinda asked, finding it hard to tear her eyes away from Tim for even a second.

'Oh, seven or eight days I should think. There's no particular hurry, is there?'

'No, no. I'm in no hurry,' Corinda said.

'Before we go outside there is just one thing. Business.' He took a folded piece of paper from the inside pocket of his suit. 'Arabella told me of your decision. I mean, that you want to leave the island and come to England. This is just a formal document acknowledging that. We have to put it on file. The status of the legacy will then be changed. Though Arabella and I are still responsible for your trust fund we are no longer your legal guardians.'

'I see,' Corinda said, hardly hearing a word he said. She was too busy watching the way his lips moved as he spoke. He had very white, very regular teeth. She imagined his lips sucking on her nipple and his teeth biting into it.

Tim took a pen from his pocket and uncapped it. He took the paper over to a side-table and waited, pen in hand.

'It is what you want, isn't it?' Arabella asked, interpreting Corinda's hesitation as a change of mind.

'Oh yes. Yes,' she said, hurrying over to Tim. It was not second thoughts that had rooted her to the spot but the effect Tim had on her. It was as if there was a time delay before the words actually got through to her brain. She stood beside him and took the pen from his hand. She could feel the warmth of his body against hers and had to overcome a desire to turn to him and kiss him on his smiling mouth. As she signed the bottom of the paper her hand brushed against his and she felt her whole body tremble.

'That's that then,' he said, picking up the paper. He waved it in the air to dry the ink, then returned it to his pocket. 'You have officially come of age, Ms Chaste. Congratulations.'

'Congratulations,' Arabella said, with sadness in her voice. 'Come on, let's go down to the beach.'

'This is such a beautiful place,' Tim said.

'And you're such a beautiful man,' Corinda said, tilting her head to one side as she stared at him again. She was peeping at his crotch, trying to see the outline of his penis, but the folds of material effectively hid it.

'Corinda, you'll embarrass the young man,' Arabella chided.

'Well, it's true,' Corinda said.

'Thank you; I don't believe I've ever had such a compliment before,' Tim said, though his unflappable response was betrayed by a blush that made his face turn red.

'There's plenty more where that came from,' Corinda added with a coquettish smile.

'That'll be enough of that,' Arabella said, shepherding Tim to the door. 'Behave yourself, Corinda.'

'I might,' she said. 'Then on the other hand, I might not.'

She picked up the bottle of champagne and poured herself a glass. For the first time in her life she felt free to do whatever she wanted, and she definitely intended to do exactly that.

Chapter Two

'Can I ask you a question?'

'Of course.'

'About my father?'

'I didn't really know him. My father looked after all his business. It's only when I took over the firm last year that I got involved in all this.'

They had sailed at eight in the morning. Corinda had wept on the jetty as Arabella said goodbye. On the yacht she stood at the stern as they pulled away, tears running down her cheeks as Arabella waved from the shore. Corinda had refused to move away until the island where she spent her youth had entirely disappeared from sight and the horizon was featureless, with the brilliant blue sky merging into the glittering dark green sea.

Then she had turned, conscious of turning her back on one life, and starting another.

Tim had shown her to her cabin. The boat was luxurious. Her quarters consisted of a large sitting room, and a spacious bedroom with a circular bed and an en-suite bathroom. Everything was fitted out with highly polished wood and brass detailing. The bathroom contained a shower stall, a sunken bathtub and a steam room as well as the bidet and wash basin. Then they had toured the rest of the boat, from the bridge to the engine room, Corinda noting all the details, especially the eight man crew. She examined each of them critically, but decided none of them were as attractive as Tim.

After a light lunch on the sun deck Corinda had fallen asleep for an hour, finding the excitement of it all quite tiring. Then she returned to her cabin.

Arabella had sent the details of her sizes to London. On the island Corinda had few clothes and, though she had insisted on bringing them all with her, she was delighted to find that Tim Morrison's secretary had been delegated to buy her several outfits for use on the boat. Tonight, Tim told her, they would have a formal dinner and, as she wanted to look her best, she spent the rest of the afternoon trying on her new wardrobe.

The drawers in the bedroom contained lingerie in white, black, and pink silk; there were panties, bras and slips. In the wardrobes hung dresses, haute couture creations from the best designers. There were shoes and boots in matching colours, and little handbags and belts that had been carefully coordinated with the outfits. Corinda tried on each one, hardly able to believe how they changed her appearance. On the island, naked or with a bright silk wrap, Corinda had been a young girl. In the full-length mirror, swathed in red, dark blue or black silk, her breasts tightly confined, she had become a woman.

She finally chose black, but not before she'd tried on everything in the wardrobe and drawers, and experimented with the hoard of make-up she found in the bathroom. Arabella had given her basic training in applying cosmetics, but on the island there was nothing like the variety of products she found neatly arranged here.

Now she stood on the aft deck looking at the wake of the propellers as they churned up the phosphorescent plankton. The dress fitted her perfectly, clinging to the tightly pronounced curves of her body, her deep cleavage displayed by its plunging neckline, though its knee-length skirt was more modest. With her tanned legs she decided against tights but, for the first time in her life, she wore high heels, though she found them uncomfortable. She had hardly worn shoes at all on the island, let alone these spike-heeled examples, and they were going to take some time to get used to. At the moment she tottered about on them precariously whenever she forgot to take tiny steps. She was determined to get used to them, however. She had noticed how they shaped and firmed the muscles of her calves and buttocks. It was all part of becoming a woman, a perfect adult.

Tim Morrison sat in a steamer chair with his feet up. He watched Corinda intently, hardly able to believe that the elegant, beautiful woman who stood looking over the stern rail was the same urchin he had seen on the island. He didn't think he had ever seen a more beautiful female. Her blonde hair cascaded over her tanned shoulders and caught the light as it moved, her face dominated by large blue eyes. It wasn't only her beauty that was appealing but her attitude; she bubbled over with life, unable and unwilling to quell her delight and excitement at what lay ahead of her.

'Would you like another glass of champagne?' he asked, refilling his own from a bottle resting in a bucket of ice on a small table at his side.

'I don't think I should,' she said. 'I'm not really used to it.'

'So what do you want to know about your father?'

'Well, Arabella explained a bit about the legacy. But I don't really understand.' She turned to look at him.

'What did she tell you?'

'She said my father was upset about what had happened to my mother. About what two men had done to her.'

'Yes, that's right. As I said, my own father dealt with him then. But I read the file. There were newspaper cuttings...'

'So what happened?'

'I'm not sure this is the time...'

'Please.'

'Your mother was raped by two men. She put up quite a fight. They hurt her very badly. She died from her injuries. It was a terrible thing. Naturally your father, with all his wealth, wanted to protect you in some way. So he decided to have you sent away to the island with Arabella as a way of guarding you from men for as long as he could. Obviously, once you came of age his wishes no longer had any legal force.'

'Did he think men would want to rape me?'

'I think he was scared of that, yes. Apparently he loved your mother very much. He never got over her death.'

'I see,' Corinda said thoughtfully.

A servant in a white linen jacket appeared from the large glass doors that led into the dining room. 'Excuse me, Mr Morrison. If you are ready, dinner is served.'

'Oh, we're ready. I'm starving. Must be the sea air,' Corinda said with childlike delight.

Tim got to his feet. He took her arm and led her through the doors, matching his own steps to her necessarily diminutive ones. Another waiter stood behind a chair at the round dining table. As she approached he drew it out for her. She giggled.

'Do they always do that?'

'In most restaurants, yes.'

'I've never been to a restaurant.' The waiter pushed the chair back in as Corinda sat down. 'I've got a lot to learn. I know about all this though.' She waved at the array of cutlery, crockery and crystal glasses that formed two place settings on the table. 'Start on the outside and work in, right?'

'Absolutely.'

'God, these shoes are killing me.'

'Take them off, I don't mind.'

'No. I'm going to suffer. The sooner I get used to them the better. Don't you think they make my legs look wonderful?' Corinda leapt to her feet, pirouetted on her toes and wriggled the tight black skirt up over her hips, until her thighs were revealed.

Tim blushed. He could see the crotch of her black panties.

'What's the matter? Don't I look good?'

Tim could see the waiter staring at her too and gestured for him to leave. Reluctantly the waiter sidled out.

'You look marvellous. It's just that...' He couldn't think of what to say.

Corinda pulled her skirt down. 'I'm sorry, I didn't mean to embarrass you,' she said, sitting down again.

'You're very uninhibited, that's all. I'm not used to it.'

'There's nothing wrong with that, is there?'

'Well, I suppose being alone with women on the island it's been very different for you. But with men around you're going to have to be a little bit more careful.'

'Careful of what? Is there something wrong with my body? You have to tell me if there is.'

'Not as far as I can see. You're a very beautiful young woman, Corinda. That's the problem really. You see it's not usual to be quite so,' he searched for the right word, 'forward.'

The door from the kitchen opened slowly, and the waiter poked his head around tentatively to see if he was allowed back in. Tim made it clear that he was. 'Let's eat shall we?'

The two waiters served a delicious dinner; freshly caught sea bass, followed by locally bought lamb roasted in wild thyme and garlic.

Tim watched Corinda as she ate. She seemed to approach everything she did with gusto, displaying a hearty appetite for life as well as the food. She asked him questions about London, about where she would live and what she would do. She had taken A-levels on the island and was qualified for university. A place had been arranged for her at Cambridge but she would have three months in London first. Her father's penthouse in Edwardes Square, Kensington, had been redecorated and refurnished for her.

She was excited by the prospect of being able to buy clothes for herself. But that was only one high spot among so many. There was the theatre, the cinema, restaurants and learning to drive. And, of course, men. Wall to wall men, in every possible shape and size. She wondered if they would all be as good-looking as Tim. She remembered the boy in the vineyard and as the waiter served dessert, a miraculous concoction of meringue, whipped cream and ice cream decorated with marron glace, she wondered what Tim would look like stripped to the waist.

'Are the women in London all very beautiful?' she asked.

'Some are,' he replied. He told the waiter they would like coffee served at the table.

'And the men? Are they all as handsome as you?'

Tim laughed. 'You're not supposed to say that.'

'Why not?'

16

'Because the relationship between a man and a woman is a game. You have to pretend.'

'Pretend what?'

'When you first meet a man you like, it's sort of customary to pretend you don't necessarily find him attractive.'

'And does he do the same?'

'No. He has to tell the woman how lovely he thinks she is.'

'So he can tell me I'm beautiful but I can't tell him that same thing?'

'Yes. At least until you get to know him.'

'That's silly. Why?'

'I suppose it's part of a courtship ritual. Women are supposed to be the hunted and men the hunter.'

'But if I want to have sex with a man shouldn't I say so right from the beginning. I mean, I'd love to have sex with you.'

Tim almost choked on his meringue.

Corinda pushed her plate away. The waiter brought in the coffee, and poured it from a large silver pot into small white cups decorated with a gold rim.

'I don't see what's wrong with that. If you were married it would be different but you're not, are you?'

'No - it's just...' He stopped himself. It occurred to him that what Corinda was saying was true. What was wrong with a woman being as forthright as a man? It was only a matter of social convention.

'I know I'm very naive. I'm bound to be, aren't I? Perhaps I'm not a very good judge because I've seen so few men, but I do think you're very good-looking. God, just saying that makes my nipples go all hard.' Quite unselfconsciously she touched the palm of her right hand against her breasts through the tight black silk.

'You definitely shouldn't do that,' Tim said sternly.

'What?' Corinda wasn't even aware of what she had done.

'Touch yourself like that in front of other people.'

Corinda looked alarmed. 'Really?'

'No. It's regarded as immodest.'

'Oh,' Corinda said, catching on quickly. 'I wouldn't have done it if the waiter was still here. I know that much. But I thought, with just the two of us. There's nothing wrong with that is there?'

Tim was torn between his sense of duty, passed down from father to son in *loco parentis*, and his feelings as a man. Not surprisingly Corinda was unlike any girl - any woman, since officially that's what she now was - he had ever met. Besides being exceptionally beautiful, she had an openness in her manner and a profound sensuality which attracted him more strongly than anything ever had before. He found he was unable to take his eyes off her.

'Let's go through to the other cabin, shall we? We'll be more comfortable in there,' he said.

Leaving the table he guided her up a short flight of stairs to the spectacular stateroom on the upper deck, its large windows affording panoramic views over the seascape. A circular banquette, upholstered in red silk, was built into the rear bulkhead facing glass doors that opened out on to a small terrace, immediately above the one they had been on earlier. Outside an almost full moon lit the sea with an eerie glow that made the waves look as if they had been burnished with platinum. Huge cumulus clouds scudded across the sky, and were lit dramatically as they passed over the face of the moon.

Tim closed the terrace doors against a freshening breeze. Where an hour before the ocean had been perfectly smooth, it was now distinctly choppy.

'Would you like a brandy?' he asked Corinda, who had sat curled up on the sofa with her legs tucked underneath her.

'No. I've had just enough to feel delicious. The wine was stronger than I'm used to on the island.'

'The local wine?'

'Yes. Arabella said it was good for me.'

'It is.'

'But I don't want to get drunk. Not now. Not here. Come and sit next to me.'

He sat down beside her. 'This is difficult for me, Corinda,' he said seriously, unable to stop himself looking at the way the silk skirt had ridden up her thighs.

'Do you know you've got dimples in your cheeks? They get deeper when you smile. Smile for me.'

He did, weakly.

'This right one is bigger.' She touched his cheek with her finger. He had an almost irresistible desire to kiss her. He held himself back.

'I was saying that this is difficult,' he insisted.

'Why difficult?'

'Because for the last year since my father died, I've been your legal guardian.'

'You've got lovely eyes.'

'Be serious.'

'That's serious.'

'I want you to understand what I'm trying to say. You're a gorgeous woman but in some ways I have come to look on you as my daughter.'

'Oh, Mr Morrison, you know I'm not your daughter. I'm eighteen now. I can decide for myself what I want. You said that on the island and the truth is, the absolute truth is, I want to have sex with you.'

She had turned to look directly into his eyes. Hers sparkled with excitement.

'But don't you see, that's only because I'm the first man you've seen.'

'So?'

'So it would be taking advantage of you; taking advantage of my position of trust.'

Corinda got to her feet. There was a glass cocktail cabinet built into the corner of the stateroom; all the bottles and glasses fitted into custom-built housing to stop them rolling around in a heavy sea. Folding down the glass front Corinda took out a teardrop-shaped bottle of Otard XO brandy and poured a large measure into a brandy balloon. She inhaled the strong aroma appreciatively, then handed the glass to Tim.

'Here, it'll help you relax,' she said. Turning her back on him, she reached around to the zip of the dress and pulled it down. She peeled the shoulder straps over her arms and wriggled her hips until the dress fell to the floor. 'Sorry,' she said, 'but it was getting uncomfortable. I'm not used to tight clothes.' She picked up the black silk and folded it neatly over the end of the sofa. 'Oh that feels so much better.' She sat next to him again.

Tim gulped a large mouthful of brandy, then put the glass down on the yew coffee table in front of the banquette. He couldn't help staring at the camber of her breasts, selling up from the lacy black cups of the plunge-cut bra. He couldn't help glancing down to her lap where the thong-cut black panties clung so tightly to the curve of her pubic bone, before disappearing between her legs. He felt his cock beginning to unfurl.

'Anyway, you're not the first man I've seen. There was a boy on the island. I used to watch him working in the vineyards. It was always so hot he used to strip down to his shorts. He looked so strong. I loved the way the sweat ran down his broad back. I could see his spine. I used to watch him for hours.' Corinda stretched back, resting her head against the cushions.

'At night I used to imagine what it would be like if he crept into my room. How I'd peel off his shorts... It always made me so wet.'

'Corinda, you shouldn't...'

She reached up to put a finger to his lips to silence him. 'But last night it wasn't that boy I was thinking about. It was you.' She slid her hand down the front of his shirt, wrapping her fingers around his silk tie. 'Oh, Mr Morrison, you don't know what it feels like. It hurts, it aches like there's a great void inside me.'

'Corinda, I can't...' he picked the brandy glass up and took another gulp. 'It would be a breach of trust.'

'I knew it,' she said brusquely. 'I'm not beautiful at all, am I? I'm probably quite plain. You were just flattering me because of my father.'

'Corinda, you're gorgeous.'

'Well then,' she said decisively. 'Oh damn. Excuse me, but this thing is killing me.' She was used to soft full-cup bras. The underwired cups she was wearing dug into her flesh. As if it were the most natural thing in the world - which of course it was for her - she reached behind her back, unhooked the bra, and threw it aside. Her breasts quivered at their freedom. Her dark red nipples were already erect, standing out like golf tees. 'That's better.'

'I suppose it's no good me telling you you're being immodest again,' Tim said, feeling his cock hardening rapidly. He could not tear his eyes away from the spectacle of her voluptuous bosom.

'Mr Morrison, I thought we'd been through all that. I wouldn't dream of stripping off in front of strangers. But you're not a stranger, are you? You just said, you feel like my father.'

'At this moment I couldn't feel less like your father,' he said. 'That's the trouble.'

'Trouble?'

'Corinda, I don't think you understand men at all. We have certain...' he searched for the right word, 'reactions when we see a beautiful naked woman.'

'Oh God, I know all about that,' she said scornfully. 'I'm not that naive. I've done A-level biology. When a man becomes excited blood flows into his penis. It's called engorgement. His penis becomes tumescent which allows him to insert it into the vagina of a female.'

'Exactly.' Tim was blushing again.

'You see. I know the theory. Then the man thrusts up and down and ejaculates his semen. The semen swims up inside the vagina to meet the ovum. It's quite simple.'

'And very complicated,' Tim added.

'But you're not engorged now, are you?'

'Of course I am. Just look at you.'

'What, just looking at me like this makes it happen?'

'I told you; you're very attractive. You've got beautiful breasts, and those long legs... I think you really should get dressed.'

Corinda ignored him. 'This is great. You mean you've got a hard penis now, just because I took my bra off?'

He looked as though he wanted to say more; that it also involved her long blonde hair, her finely sculpted features, the soft creaminess of her flesh, the way her body moved and those big blue luminescent eyes. But instead he just said, 'Yes.'

'Can I see it?'

'What?'

'Can I see your penis? I've never seen one, Mr Morrison. I've never even seen a soft one, let alone one that's - what's the right word? Erect?'

'Corinda, that's what I've been trying to explain to you. It wouldn't be right.'

'Not right? It's only a question of curiosity, isn't it?'

'No, it is not. I told you sex is much more complicated. If I undress, if I show you my...' he hesitated to use the word, '...cock, it will make me even more excited. It's not like a biology lesson. I might not be able to control myself.'

Corinda looked puzzled. 'I'm not sure I understand that.'

Tim tried to think of a way to explain. 'When you were talking about the boy you used to watch?'

'Yes.'

'You imagined seeing him naked?'

'Yes.'

'And that excited you, sexually I mean?'

'Yes.'

'So wouldn't you have been even more excited if he'd actually been there? Wouldn't you have wanted to do more than just look?'

'Of course.' Corinda laughed. 'I'd have eaten him alive.'

'Well then, it's exactly the same for me.'

Corinda thought about that for a moment. The clouds outside had thickened considerably, blocking out the moon and there was nothing to see through the windows now but the superstructure of the yacht. Everything beyond was pitch black. The sea was choppier too and, though the boat was fitted with stabilisers, it was beginning to roll slightly from side to side.

'I suppose you're right,' she said gloomily. Suddenly her face lit up again, a new thought having occurred to her. 'But there's nothing to say you have to control yourself, is there? We can have sex. We can do it right now.'

'No,' Tim said firmly. 'I can't Corinda, I thought I'd explained.'

'You said it would be breaking a trust. But that's silly. I'm eighteen now. I can make my own mind up about what I want, can't I? I really think you're handsome. I really want to have sex with you. I really want to do it now.'

'That's not the point.' He was losing the argument with himself. His erection was rock hard and throbbing. Corinda's breasts trembled as she talked so animatedly. He desperately wanted to cup his hands around them and press his fingers into the soft, pliant flesh. 'I'm the first man you've ever met. It's natural you should feel this way about me. But once you've seen other men you'll be able to pick and choose. You only want me because it's convenient.'

'I've seen the crew and the waiters. I don't want to have sex with them.' That wasn't strictly true. Had Tim not been there Corinda would have been very interested in one of the waiters. He had short curly black hair and the way he'd looked at her, particularly the way he looked down the front of her dress as he'd served her dinner, had excited her.

Corinda got to her feet. She was still wearing the black high heels. She looked at her reflection in the terrace windows. Looking over her shoulder she could see her tight buttocks parted by the black thong of the panties. She cupped her breasts in her hands, then fed the left nipple up towards her mouth, until she could catch it between her teeth. She pinched it lightly then repeated the process with the other breast.

'I've been able to do that since I was sixteen,' she said proudly. 'Is your penis still tumescent, Mr Morrison?'

'Of course it is.'

She let go of her tits and sat on the edge of the coffee table right in front of him, leaning forward until her breasts brushed her thighs. 'How long will it take to get to England?'

'Six or seven days.'

'Don't you think,' she said, taking a different approach, 'that it's really your duty to teach me something about men before we get there. I mean, imagine what it would be like for me in London. All those men. All those tumescent penises... or is it penii? I could go completely wild with lust. You wouldn't want that on your conscience, would you Mr Morrison?'

'No, of course not.'

'Well then.' She dropped her hands to his knees and caressed them.

'Oh God, Corinda, why are you doing this to me?' He was weakening. What she said was perfectly true. In London she would be prey to all kinds of unscrupulous men. What if she let lust overcome good judgment? She was, after all, a very wealthy heiress. The first man who took an interest in her might well be doing it for all the wrong reasons. At least he could trust himself to have the right motives. Once she'd had a little experience she wouldn't be so likely to dash into a reckless affair.

'Doing what?'

Even this rationalisation didn't entirely convince him. He hadn't the slightest idea what he should do. 'Tempting me. You're so beautiful.'

The boat rolled to one side quite noticeably. Corinda grabbed Tim's legs to stop herself sliding along the coffee table. There was a flash of lightning and a loud clap of thunder. Almost immediately heavy rain began to batter at the windows.

'Please let me see, Mr Morrison. It's not fair telling me you're hard and not letting me see.' She pouted with her best poor-little-rich-girl expression.

Tim stood up decisively. He stripped off his cream linen jacket and his beige silk tie. Corinda's eyes were level with the flies of his trousers and he could see her studying the bulge underneath them. He kicked off his slip-on shoes and pulled off his white silk socks.

'Is this really want you want?'

'I don't think I've ever wanted anything more in my entire life,' she said earnestly, meaning every word of it.

'There's a zip at the front,' he said. 'Pull it down.' Corinda extended her right hand. She found the metal tongue of the zip and pulled it down rather awkwardly, the protrusion underneath made it difficult. Finally she got it all the way down, the material parting to reveal white boxer shorts. Without waiting to be given permission she fished inside. She supposed she would never forget that first touch. Her fingers fell on a sword of flesh so hot she almost snatched her hand away. But she didn't. Instead she curled her fist around it and pulled it out through the fly. She stared at it. It was throbbing visibly. She felt her own sex fluttering with sensations too, quite unlike any she'd felt in bed with Arabella. It was much larger than she'd imagined, larger even than the dildo Arabella had given her two nights before. The tip, what she knew from her biology textbooks was called the glans, was smooth and pink and divided from the shaft by a distinct rim. The shaft itself was more gnarled, covered with veins and, towards the base, quite thick blond hair.

Tim pulled his trousers and pants down together and stepped out of them. He stripped off his shirt. His chest was hairless apart from a few wisps around his nipples. 'Well, there you are,' he said. 'Have you got what you wanted?'

His cock stood up almost vertically. She saw its pulse. There was a slit at the tip and a tear of sticky fluid was leaking from it. Now he was naked she could see his balls too. They were large and heavy, his scrotum covered in curly hair.

'It's wet,' Corinda said. Then she remembered; a man produced a secretion when he became excited just like a woman did. 'Cowper's fluid,' she said almost to herself. She wrapped her hand around his shaft again and squeezed it. The glans expanded like a little balloon. 'It's so hard. Like a bone.'

'Yes. It's caused by looking at you.'

'It's big too. I didn't think it would be so big. I can't believe it's going to fit inside me. Mind you I thought that about the dildo.'

'The dildo?' Tim said, astonished.

'Yes, Arabella bought me one for my birthday. I guess she thought it would be good practice.'

'Did you use it?'

'It was nice. But it wasn't as big as this and it certainly wasn't so hot. The semen comes out here, right?' She poked the slit of the urethra with her fingernail.

'Yes.'

'Show me that now then,' she said.

The boat lurched hard to one side. Rain was falling heavily now, driving against the windows noisily.

He laughed. 'It's not like pressing a button,' he told her.

The textbooks had explained the mechanics of copulation but had been light on detail when it came to the cause of ejaculation. Corinda had assumed it was something akin to having to pee. 'Haven't you got enough then?' she asked.

'Enough what?'

'Enough semen. How many times do you ejaculate per day?'

'I think you've got the wrong idea. A man only ejaculates when he's stimulated.'

'Stimulated?'

'When his penis is rubbed in a woman's sex or in her hand or...' He stopped himself from saying what he wanted to say.

'Go on,' Corinda urged.

'Her mouth.'

'Mouth?' Corinda exclaimed. 'I can put it in my mouth?' Before he could reply she dipped her head, opened her mouth wide and slipped her lips around his cock. She felt it twitch against her tongue. 'My God,' she said pulling away, 'that feels so good.' She repeated the exercise, before he could protest, swallowing more of him this time. As she pulled away he saw her studying his cock intently. 'Will you ejaculate now?' she asked, without taking her eyes off him.

'If you do that enough I might.'

'Aren't I doing it right?'

'Of course you are, but it isn't instant.'

'Shall I do it again?'

'No.'

'Show me how to rub it with my hand.'

'All right.' Tim was resigned to the fact that he clearly had no choice but to give the girl what she so earnestly wanted. 'Like this.' He made a ring of his thumb and forefinger and slipped it over the top of his cock. Slowly he moved it up and down as she watched closely.

'I've got it.' She pulled his hand away and replaced it with her own. But she squeezed much harder than he had and he moaned. 'Is that wrong?' she asked.

'No, it's right. Very right.'

'Does it make you want to ejaculate?'

'Yes.'

'Oh good. Do it then.' She moved her hand up and down still faster. 'Let me see it.'

'No,' he said, grabbing her wrist.

At exactly that moment the boat lurched to one side. Tim lost his balance and fell back on the sofa. Corinda leaped on top of him, pressing her body against his.

'Oh that's good. Your body's so hard. Not just your penis. I mean all of it. So different from a woman.'

'What do you mean?'

Corinda was about to tell him about Arabella, when she stopped herself. She didn't want to get into all that now and she had a feeling he might be shocked. 'Women are soft,' she said instead. The strength of his body, in contrast to the melting softness of Arabella, excited her just as she'd imagined it would. She pressed her navel against his penis, and felt its hardness and heat boring into her. Her clitoris throbbed so strongly it was her turn to moan.

'You certainly are,' he said. It was at that moment that he lost the battle with his conscience. He looked into her eyes and found himself moving his mouth to hers. They kissed hungrily, greedily, writhing together as their tongues danced around each other.

'Oh God, Corinda,' Tim managed to say.

'Can I do the other thing now?' she asked.

'What other thing?'

'Caress your penis with my sex? That will make you ejaculate, won't it?'

'Yes.'

'Let me then. Let me do it, Mr Morrison, please.'

There was a flash of lightning which lit up the sky, then a clap of thunder that seemed to come from directly overhead. The boat yawed, dived into the trough of a wave, then climbed up to the following crest. Another flash of lightning forked into the sea, the thunder rattling the glasses in the cocktail cabinet.

'It's romantic, isn't it?' Corinda said, thinking of the storm in Wuthering Heights. The important thing was that she had her Heathcliff.

She managed to scramble to her feet. She took hold of the waistband of the black panties and pulled them down her long legs, her eyes watching Tim's reaction. How many times in the future would she peel away the final layer of protection and expose herself for a man? She saw his cock pulse as his eyes lighted on her downy pubic hair. It hid little. He would be able to see the crease of her labia. She had never felt herself as wet as this, even under Arabella's expert ministrations. She was sure her juices were running down her thighs.

'You are going to let me, aren't you?' she said, kneeling at his side. 'You are going to show me how to make you ejaculate, aren't you Mr Morrison?' She lifted her thigh and straddled his hips before he could answer.

With her legs spread apart he could see her sex clearly. Her pubic hair did not extend over her delicate labia and he could see every detail. It was glistening wet. 'You're really beautiful,' he said, gazing up at her mouth-watering breasts.

'Come on, Mr Morrison. It's time for the next lesson in my education.' Slowly she eased herself down on his cock. She felt it nosing between her sex lips. It butted into her clitoris, giving her a sensation so sharp it made her moan again. Very gently she rubbed herself against it, feeling it push her clitoris up and down. She could hear her heart beating. His cock was inches from her vagina, seconds away from penetrating her, from filling her, from turning something she had dreamt of so many times into a reality.

This time the flash of lightning seemed to be centred on the ship. There was an enormous crack and the lights went out. With no moon outside the stateroom was plunged into darkness. At the same time the boat lurched violently to one side, the floor at almost a forty-degree angle. Everything that was not secured was pitched against the side wall. As the boat swung in the opposite direction Corinda was knocked off balance and thrown back onto the coffee table. She heard a dull thud and felt a sharp stab of pain as her head rapped against the corner, and she rolled onto the carpeted floor.

She could see nothing. She reached up to her head and was alarmed to feel the warmth and wetness of blood. As she tried to get to her feet the boat pitched again, throwing her to one side.

'Tim!' she shouted.

'Corinda, are you all right?'

The emergency lighting had kicked in, bathing the stateroom in a shadowy, dim light. She saw Tim trying to struggle up off the sofa, his body a curious metallic white in the strange light. Then another flash of lightning and another explosion plunged the room into darkness again as a clap of thunder, so loud it hurt the ears, crashed around them. The noise of the engines, unnoticed by virtue of its continuous drone, changed dramatically. Instead of their regular thrum they stuttered, then died. Almost immediately the boat lost headway, slewing around in the increasingly mountainous sea. A huge wave hit them broadside. Corinda heard glass breaking but the stateroom windows were left intact.

As the boat pitched another wave tried to overwhelm it, then a third, even larger than the other two, and the ship wallowed. There was a huge crash and the windows of the terrace doors were smashed open; cold salt water washing over Corinda's naked body.

'Tim! Tim!' she screamed.

She heard no reply, but it was difficult to hear anything with the windows gone, except the roar of the wind and rain and pounding ocean. Suddenly there was another more ominous sound; a long metallic clang. The whole ship juddered, its movement momentarily arrested. Corinda knew instinctively what had happened. They'd hit some underwater obstacle, ripping open the steel hull.

Another grinding sound followed. The huge waves picked the yacht off whatever it had grounded on and tossed it to one side. Corinda was thrown against the bulkhead, but this time the yacht did not right itself. Instead it began to sink.

Corinda knew she was going to die. As water poured into the stateroom, flooding over her, as she fought what she knew was a losing battle to keep her head above it, she could only think about the irony of the fact that, had catastrophe struck only a few seconds later she would have lost her virginity as well as her life. Now, she would die never having known what it was like to have a man deep inside her.

Chapter Three

It was so black there was no difference between having her eyes open and having them shut. She blinked several times but the situation did not improve. She wondered if she had gone blind. The thought sent a chill through her. She held her hand up in front of her face but, as hard as she tried, she could see nothing.

Having her eyes open increased the pounding headache responsible for waking her. There was a large and tender bump on the back of her head. She fingered it gingerly and was relieved to find it was not bleeding any more.

She was sure that, wherever she was, she was not on the boat. There was no lateral motion and no pitching, nor the sound of the sea. In fact there was no sound at all.

'Tim!' she cried. 'Tim, where are you?' There was no reply.

Groping around with her hands, moving slowly for fear of exacerbating the headache, Corinda tried to work out where she was. As far as she could tell she was lying on a perfectly normal double bed. The room was warm and she was naked, with a single cotton sheet folded over her body. Carefully she sat up. The hammering in her head reached a new pitch, then subsided. Swinging her legs off the bed she felt a soft carpet under her feet. She groped to the left and felt a bedside table and a lamp. Finding the switch just under the bulb, she screwed her eyes tightly shut and pushed it on. Nothing happened. Even with her eyes shut she would have been aware of light from the lamp. Tentatively she opened her eyes again. The room was as black as before.

A wave of despair overcame her. She was blind. The crack on her head had damaged the neuron pathways from her eyes to her brain. Her only hope was the damage might not be permanent.

She got to her feet. The pitch of her headache increased, then settled to a dull, less intrusive throb. Moving forward with her hands out in front of her she explored the room, trying to get a picture of it in her mind. She found a wall and groped her way along it. As far as she could tell the room was furnished normally. There were pictures on the walls; a bookcase full of books and, she discovered by stubbing her toe on it, a large and comfortable armchair. What was unusual, however, was that she could find no windows and though there was a doorway, it was closed by what seemed to be a slatted metal shutter instead of a door.

She found no other bed. She was alone.

She discovered a jug of water and a glass on the bedside table and, with difficulty, poured some. She found she was very thirsty, having consumed, no doubt, a great deal of salt water.

Lying back on the bed, the headache almost gone, she began to wonder what had happened. Obviously the storm had pushed the yacht onto some rocks and it had foundered. The last thing she remembered was the water pouring into the stateroom. Perhaps, she thought, she was actually dead, and that this strange room and her blindness was the prelude to the afterlife. She dismissed the thought as silly. Apart from the blindness and the bump on her head she felt perfectly normal and very much alive.

She thought about Tim again. Very slowly and gently she began rubbing her breasts. Her nipples were soft and had retracted. But as she circled her palm from one to the other she felt them responding, popping up instantly, hard and tingling. They sent messages directly to her sex, and she felt her clitoris pulse.

In this strange environment, in circumstances she did not understand, there was something comforting in her body's habitual responses to this familiar stimulation. Taking her left nipple between thumb and forefinger she pinched. She brought her other hand up to the right nipple, her arms crossed, and pinched both nipples simultaneously. She pinched for a second time, using her fingernails to produce a sharper sensation. The double impact of pain tinted with pleasure made her gasp. Her clitoris pulsed more strongly, as if trying to draw attention to itself.

For the moment she ignored her nether regions. Taking her nipples firmly in her fingers she lifted her breasts by them. Then she gripped the flesh and began kneading it like dough, squeezing and pummelling to produce wave after wave of pleasure.

She had not intended to masturbate. The exercise had started as a means of reassurance, an assertion of certainty amidst all the uncertainty that surrounded her; the equivalent of wrapping herself in a security blanket. But her body began to have other ideas. With her legs closed she felt herself pressing her thighs together to put pressure on her clitoris.

Corinda rolled onto her stomach. She brought her knees up under her, stuck her bottom into the air, but kept her forehead resting on the sheet. Spreading her legs apart she sent her hand down over her flat stomach to her soft pubic hair.

Normally in this position she would have been able to watch as her fingers explored the crease of her labia, but she could see nothing. The deprivation of one sense, however, seemed to increase the sensitivity of the others. She heard a slight squelching sound as her middle finger delved between her nether lips, her sex already liquid. The aroma of arousal seemed stronger; a sweet musky smell. But it was the sense of touch that was the greatest beneficiary of her visual incapacity. Her clitoris was tingling. It responded to gentle probing with pulses of pleasure that made her moan.

She tried to bring herself back under control, taking her hand away. But it was too late. She ran both her hands up the backs of her thighs and over her taut buttocks, spreading her fingers wide to encompass as much of them as she could. She pulled them apart and could feel her vagina opening.

Suddenly she straightened up. She remembered Tim. How long ago was it that she straddled over him in exactly this position, her knees either side of his hips, his penis nudging her labia? She tried to imagine what it would have been like. The penetration of the dildo had shocked and delighted her. But that had been cold and inanimate. Tim's cock would have been hot and throbbing, and alive. She could see it in her mind's eye; the smooth glans leaking a tear of fluid.

'Oh Tim, Tim,' she said aloud. She moved her right hand back down to her sex and quickly located her clitoris. It trembled against her finger. With practised deftness she established a rhythm that matched the unconscious tempo that already seemed to have invaded her; the tempo of her own sexuality. Her body responded with a jolt of pleasure. 'Tim,' she gasped, wanting to hear his name.

In the absolute darkness it was easy to imagine him lying between her thighs, the expression on his face torn between a worried guilt and an overriding excitement. It was easy to imagine herself sliding back on him until his cock was settled into the little mouth of her vagina. She moved her left hand over her buttocks until her fingertips nudged that very spot. She tried to remember how the dildo had felt as Arabella pushed it into her body; how it had parted her silky wet flesh as it filled her. She pushed two fingers into her body, then added a third, pushing all three as far as they would go. She wanted to feel her sex stretching to accommodate them, as she knew she would have been stretched by the thickness of Tim's erection.

Almost immediately she felt her body flood with even sharper sensations, as though she was changing to a higher gear. This was not like her usual masturbation ritual, where she would often tease herself for some time, able to keep her orgasm bubbling near the surface but never allowing it to escape; not at least until she was ready. This orgasm could not be controlled. The images her mind was playing in the total darkness, like pictures on a cinema screen, were too strong, her imagination too vivid. She pushed her fingers in and out of her sex, in imitation of Tim's cock. How would it feel when it ejaculated? Would his semen be hot? Would she be able to feel it splattering into the deepest recesses of her sex? Would she feel its wetness, trickling down the walls of her vagina?

'Oh Tim, Tim, Tim,' she cried. Her body went rigid as her orgasm broke over her. It rushed through her, sweeping her up and away to another place where there was nothing but pure, unadulterated pleasure.

She was a long time coming back. When the exquisite feelings finally released their hold on her she dropped back onto the bed. Lying on her side, she curled into a tight foetal ball and fell into a deep, apparently dreamless, sleep.

'I want to know the truth.' The voice was oddly high-pitched and reedy.

'Get me out of this, you bastard,' Tim said bravely.

'Casting aspersions on my parentage seems to me to be a little unwise considering your current predicament, my friend.'

It was true. Tim was in no position to be hurling insults. In fact he was completely helpless and totally vulnerable. He was bound securely, spread-eagled in the middle of a giant wheel made from tubular steel, the two hoops of metal joined together by a series of struts placed at regular intervals around their circumference. Hanging from four of the struts were short chains attached to padded leather cuffs. And it was these which held Tim's wrists and ankles so securely, stretching his body across the device, leaving him unable to do more than writhe ineffectively against them.

Though he had no memory of how he got there, Tim had regained consciousness in this position. He was naked, as he had been on the yacht. It was easy to see the predicament he was in since the room which housed the wheel, to which he was bound, was completely lined with mirrors. They were not just on all four walls but on the floor and ceiling too. He could see his tethered body from every angle. Every strained muscle and stretched sinew stared back at him from wherever he cared to look.

He had only been conscious for a few minutes when a door set into the wall of mirrors in front of him had opened and the man entered. He was one of the oddest looking men Tim had ever seen. His head was shaved and shone under the lights, as though oiled and polished, and he had a bull-neck. He was stripped to the waist and wore leather riding breeches and boots. His barrel chest was deep and covered with a thick mat of hair which was completely white. He had a wide nose that looked as though it had been broken in at least two places, and small ears that stood out at right angles. His eyes were small too, and a bright pinkish grey. The colour was even more pronounced in contrast to the complexion of his face which, like his body, was an alabaster white.

'I want to know the truth,' he repeated. 'That is all.' He smiled, revealing several gold teeth.

'Why have you brought me here?' Tim asked, struggling against his bonds.

'Young man, it is for me to ask the questions. I want you to tell me what your cargo was. That is not too difficult, is it?' Though his English was perfect he spoke with a heavy accent. 'How rude of me. We have not been introduced. My name is Constantine Evangelos Stephanikis. And you are Timothy Morrison. I found your papers. Now just tell me what cargo you were carrying on that fine vessel.'

'Cargo? What are you talking about? We didn't have a cargo.'

'What a pity. No jewels? Money? Gold?'

'No. Nothing. We were on our way to England.' Tim had no idea who this man was. He had heard stories of pirates operating in the Mediterranean, and was beginning to wonder if what had befallen the yacht was entirely accidental.

'And how many females?' the Greek asked.

'Just one. Is she alive?' Tim asked anxiously.

'Oh yes.' The man smiled broadly. 'She is very much alive. And enjoying my hospitality.'

Tim suddenly had visions of Corinda stripped and bound as he was. 'You bastard. If you hurt her I'll kill you.'

Constantine laughed. 'I'm shaking in my boots. Is that the right expression? Really Mr Morrison I can assure you I have no intention of hurting her. She is my only prize. I go to a great deal of trouble to get you on my humble little island. I have to send out a complex set of decoy radio markers to fool your electronic navigating systems and get your boat into exactly the right position in a very narrow channel to the south. I lay very nasty steel girders embedded in concrete on the shallow sea bed there, all at great expense. Do you imagine, having gone to all this trouble and having nothing to show for it but a young, and admittedly very beautiful girl, that I would harm her?' He laughed again. It was an almost manic sound. 'No, my friend. Your companion is completely safe. You, on the other hand, are in a much more precarious position.'

He stepped closer, until their bodies were almost touching.

'You won't get away with this,' Tim said defiantly.

This produced more laughter. 'My dear boy, I have been getting away with it, as you put it, for years. No one will stop me. If you have any foolish ideas about rescue I suggest you dismiss them now. Your yacht sunk without trace. Due to my electronic decoys your captain believed your last position to be one hundred and fifty miles north of here, and the distress signal he radioed minutes before you went down reflected that belief. That is where any search will concentrate.' He stepped back. 'So, now I want you to tell me all about my prize. What is her name? How old is she? Everything. I need the information to gain her confidence.' He smiled, the gold teeth catching the light.

'I'll tell you nothing.'

'Why did I know you would say that?' He went to the mirrored door and opened it. 'I think it's time you met Eloisa.'

A woman entered the room, wheeling a metal trolley in front of her. Her appearance was as bizarre as the Greek's. She was tall even without the high heels of her black ankle-boots, which elevated her another three or four inches so she towered over Constantine. Her head was large and she had strong features; a long straight nose, a jutting chin, big oval dark brown eyes, and hollow cheeks. Her black hair was cropped and stood up vertically on her scalp like the bristles of a brush. Her complexion was a dark coffee colour. Her body was of Amazonian proportions, her muscles hard from regular training with weights, the contours of each muscle group carved deeply into her flesh. She was wearing the skimpiest of garments; a black leather halter covered her small breasts and was attached to a wide belt around her waist, leaving her back completely bare. Another strip of leather ran down from the belt to cover her pubis and her sex. It emerged behind her, dividing into two at the top of the cleft between her large buttocks, and re-joining the belt at either side.

Tim could see every angle of her body reflected in the mirrors. By looking down at the floor he could even see the way the thong of leather cut into her sex revealing rubbery labia on either side. Her black pubes had obviously been shaved, leaving dark stubble on either side of the leather.

Eloisa closed the mirrored door, then wheeled the trolley up to Tim. The top was draped with a bright blue scarf. From the indentations in the silk there were obviously several objects lying underneath.

'Not a bad specimen,' she said. Her accent was American. She walked behind him and ran her hand down his back until she reached his buttocks. 'What do you want me to do?'

'Apparently this gentleman has decided he wishes to withhold information from me.'

Eloisa smiled a knowing smile. She had large, regular teeth. 'Well, that's just great. Time we had some fun around here.' She walked around in front of him and seized his cock in her hand. 'I don't think it's going to take too long to change his mind, do you?' She rubbed her finger against the distinct rim at the bottom of Tim's glans. To his amazement he felt his cock throb with excitement. In this position the last thing he had expected was to experience sexual excitement. He looked down at his cock. It was already beginning to swell.

'You see,' Eloisa said triumphantly, as the erection grew between her fingers. She squeezed to encourage the development while her other hand reached under the silk scarf on the trolley and came out with a long thong of leather. Expertly she looped the leather under his balls and around his rapidly expanding erection. Tying it tightly at the base of his shaft, she pulled the two loose ends around to the front. Then she twisted them over each other before stretching them down between his balls, and looped them under his scrotum and back over the shaft again, where she tied them off securely. His cock was now fully erect and straining against the leather binding, his balls spread apart by it and no less restricted, the veins and skin of his scrotum stretched taut.

Tim's reaction was as unexpected as his erection. The restraint of the leather made his cock throb wildly, and he felt an unaccountable sexual arousal.

'Look at that,' Eloisa said. 'Are you into this, bad boy?' she mocked.

'No,' he said, struggling again. 'Get me out of this.'

'Get you out of it? When you've just started having fun?' Eloisa stepped back. Like a magician completing a startling trick she whipped the silk scarf from the top of the trolley and let it fall to the floor. Tim looked down at what she had revealed. There were several straps and clips and steel instruments, a black tube moulded into the shape of an erect penis, and a short leather whip.

'So much simpler if you tell me what I want to know,' Constantine said, seeing Tim eyeing the trolley with alarm.

Tim said nothing.

Eloisa looked at the Greek. He nodded for her to continue. Without a word she picked up a short chain. Attached to each end was a miniature replica of a tiger's head, made from silver and no bigger than an acorn, its jaws bared and teeth flashing. Eloisa pinched the back of the head and Tim saw the jaws open, the inner surface of the teeth serrated with tiny metal nodules. Carefully the woman positioned one of the jaws over his left nipple.

As she allowed the teeth to clamp around the tender flesh he expected pain. Instead he experienced a wave of pleasure so intense he moaned. There was pain too, but it was so striated with pleasure he could not separate one sensation from the other. As the second clip pinched into his right nipple the feeling was renewed.

Eloisa took the chain that hung down between the two heads and pulled it out until taut. The imitation teeth bit deeper. Tim moaned for a second time, the pleasure and the pain making his cock swell against its leather bindings.

'This is almost too easy,' Eloisa said.

She let the chain drop and picked up the black phallus. Taking the top off a dark green jar she dipped the glans-shaped tip into it. The jar contained a thick white cream. Tim could have little doubt about what she was going to do with it.

'No,' he said.

'Oh yes,' Eloisa said. She was smiling, clearly enjoying his reactions.

She moved behind him but Tim could see everything she did in the mirrors. Looking down into the mirror on the floor he saw, as well as felt, her push the dildo between his buttocks.

'No, please,' he begged. The extraordinary thing was he found he didn't mean it. As the head of the phallus nosed into the puckered gate of his anus he found it created a thrill of excitement that was quite new to him. More blood coursed into his erection. Whether it was the tightness of the leather thong, or the powerlessness the bondage imposed, or the nipple clips, or the prospect of being penetrated, or all three, it had never been so hard. It was like steel.

'What are you doing to me?' he said.

'I think you know that, pretty boy,' Eloisa said. He felt the dildo test the muscle of his sphincter. It resisted initially, then relaxed and the dildo slid into him. Again he experienced that peculiar melange of pleasure and pain, though this time it was even more intense.

Eloisa circled a hand around his body and grabbed his erection, squeezing it in her fist. Letting go of the phallus she ironed her body against his back so the base of the dildo was pressed against her navel. Pushing her belly forward, the muscles of her buttocks dimpled and hard, she made the dildo slide deeper, the cream making the penetration frictionless. She moved back, allowing the dildo to slide out an inch or two, then bucked her hips again and drove it forward just as though she were a man.

'You love it don't you, pretty boy?'

He stopped himself from saying yes.

Her fist started to move up and down his cock. With her other hand she caught the chain on the nipple clips and pulled it up. A new shock of pain that translated into pulsing pleasure overwhelmed him. An electric connection seemed to have been made between his anus, his nipples and his cock; an extraordinary sensation flowed between them.

'Please,' he said, though he did not know what he wanted.

'Please what, pretty boy?'

The tip of her finger rubbed over the ridge of his glans. His cock jerked in response. He looked to his left so he could see Eloisa's body pressed against his own, her muscled legs spread apart, her leather-covered breasts crushed into his back. As he watched she sank her lips to his neck, sucking and biting. She moved her mouth up to his ear and forced her tongue into the inner whorls. It was hot and wet, and made him shudder.

Constantine Evangelos Stephanikis stood watching, his own erection straining against the confines of his leather trousers. The young man would tell him everything he wanted to know. Eloisa was an expert at her work. She had been on one of the first boats he had wrecked some years ago. She had been recruited to his staff with the promise that many of the young women, who would no doubt be shipwrecked on his island, would be consigned to her un-tender mercies. Occasionally, if the mood took her, she would take a young man too, but her preference had always been for women.

Tim's body was reeling. His nipples and anus were on fire, the pain and the pleasure melded together. His cock was so full of spunk he thought it might burst. He had never wanted to come more in his life. But he couldn't. Eloisa's touch was infuriating. Strong enough to keep him on the brink of orgasm but not strong enough to take him over it.

'Please,' he repeated, this time knowing exactly what he wanted. He wanted her to close her fist tightly around his cock, so he could fuck it. He needed to relieve the enormous pressure she had created in him, the desperate desire to come.

But Eloisa had other plans. Dropping the chain she stepped back.

'No!' he cried in alarm.

'Yes, pretty boy,' she assured him.

The dildo began to slip from his anus. Almost playfully she pushed it back with the palm of her hand, then allowed it to slip out again under its own weight. She caught it as it was finally expelled.

'Do you want to come?' she whispered in his ear, still wet from where her tongue had licked.

'Yes. Yes, please. Please let me.' His whole body ached for it.

'Too bad,' Eloisa said. He could see her in the mirror, smiling cruelly.

She moved to the side of the steel wheel. The base of the structure was slotted into two tracks set into the floor. She took hold of the two outer hoops and pulled them down. They moved smoothly on the tracks, the wheel turning. Two or three more tugs and Tim was upside down, hanging from his ankles, his head a few inches from the floor, the chain of the nipple clips now looped around his chin.

In the mirror on the ceiling he saw her go to the trolley. She picked up the leather whip.

'This is the part she enjoys,' Constantine said.

Eloisa positioned herself behind Tim. He watched as she raised the whip, her muscles tensing. He flexed as he saw her arm flash down. Instantly a stripe of searing pain exploded across his buttocks. He had expected that. What he had not expected was that the pain would turn to equally intense pleasure that coursed through his body, directly to the nerves of his cock, provoking them to new levels of arousal.

He saw Eloisa raise the whip again. A second explosion erupted in his buttocks, followed by a third and a fourth.

She changed position slightly, aiming the whip down between his open thighs. The fifth lash landed at the top of his right thigh, narrowly missing his tied balls. The sixth stroke targeted the same area on his left thigh. Then she alternated between the two; three more strokes on each.

Tim's whole body was on fire. He struggled against the bondage, not in an effort to escape, but to try and relieve the incredible need the whipping had created. It had been bad before, but not like this. He tried to fuck the air, bucking his hips. His cock was straining at the need that was mounting in him. He had read about men who were bound and whipped for sexual pleasure, but had never imagined it was something that would affect him. Not like this. He could feel each weal the whip left on his body, each distinct and separate. They sent signals of intense sexual pleasure to his cock, every nerve in his body crackling with the electric desire to ejaculate.

Hanging upside down, his cock rested against his belly. A sticky fluid leaked from the slit of his urethra. In the mirrors all around him he could see the marks Eloisa had inflicted. They seemed to be alive, pulsing, radiating heat and unbearable excitement. He saw the woman walking slowly around to face him. She knelt with her legs apart so he found himself staring into her crotch. The black leather between her legs had worked its way so far into her sex it was barely visible. He could see every detail of her engorged labia.

She leant forward and ran the tip of her tongue up along his erection. 'Would you like me to take it in my mouth?' she whispered.

'God yes. Yes...' Sweat was running off his body and pooling on the mirrored

34

floor.

She kissed the tip of his glans and he trembled. She leant back and looked up at Constantine.

'He's ready,' she said.

'Will you tell me about the girl?' Constantine asked.

It was a simple choice, Tim knew. If he told the Greek what he wanted to know Eloisa would lean forward again and slip his straining cock into her mouth. There was no other decision he could make.

'Yes. Anything.'

Constantine smiled. 'Then you will get your reward.'

Eloise held his cock with one hand. She shook it playfully from side to side then fed it into her mouth. It would not take long. She found this young man attractive. He had a large cock and a strong body. She was definitely going to spend some more time with him, when it would be his turn to please and pleasure her, or pay for the consequences of failure.

Tim shuddered as her warm wet mouth encircled his erection. He felt her tongue lick the top of his glans, then her lips closed around him and she sucked hard. He moaned loudly. His cock jerked violently, at last given the receptacle it so badly needed. He felt her thrusting forward, until he was deep in her throat and her lips were grazing his pubic hair. She pulled back slightly, sucked his glans, then sank down on him again. Her hands came up behind him and caressed the smarting weals that decorated his tortured buttocks and immediately his spunk erupted, his cock jerking violently in her mouth.

Eloisa smiled to herself. He would have to do a lot better than that when her turn came.

The noise woke her. With her heart thumping she listened intently but could not interpret what the sound was. It was certainly some sort of electric motor, a winding sound that was distinctly metallic.

Suddenly she saw a crack of light appear at the bottom of the doorway she'd found. A huge tide of relief swept over her. She was not blind!

The noise stopped. The tiny crack of light remained. After a minute or two the noise began again. The crack widened a few inches. More light flooded in. The noise stopped and the metal shutter in the doorway, being raised like a roller-blind, was halted again. It allowed her eyes to adjust to the light. Another five minutes passed before it raised again, this time opening completely, the steel rolling up into its housing.

Corinda glanced around the room. The walls were white, as were the sheets on the bed. The pictures she had found were oil paintings. They were seascapes and all featured the sun, either setting or rising, radiating a spectrum of colour from orange to ochre. There was a normal door in one corner, and the room had no windows.

Before she'd had time to take it all in a man strode into the room. Even to her inexperienced eyes his appearance was extraordinary. Despite his odd eyes and complexion the bald, bull-necked man had an aura of power about him. He was wearing dark blue slacks and a white shirt, open at the neck, a thatch of chest hair peeking out. His shoes were velvet with a gold insignia embroidered on them, and she was aware of a strong flowery cologne.

'My dear, my dear, I hope we did not startle you.'

Two young women followed him into the room, so alike physically they could have been sisters. Both were brunettes with short wavy hair and slender figures. They both wore the same style of neat white dress. They both carried trays, on one of which was a silver coffee pot, a white cup and saucer, milk jug and sugar bowl. The other bore a large basket of fruit, another of croissants and bread rolls and little bowls of butter, honey and jam. The girls put the trays down on the foot of the bed and retreated to the doorway to await further instructions.

The sight of food made Corinda realise she was very hungry. It did not occur to her for a minute to be embarrassed by her nudity.

'Constantine Evangelos Stephanikis, at your service,' the man said, sitting in the armchair. 'Please eat. The coffee is excellent. I roast the beans myself.' His eyes roamed over her naked body.

'Corinda Chaste. Pleased to meet you,' she said, taking a bite of a croissant and pouring the coffee. 'What happened to me? How did I get here?'

'I was hoping you would be able to tell us that. But first I must apologise for this rather strange environment. As you may have noticed my appearance is rather unusual; my eyes, my complexion. I have a rare allergy to sunlight. If I expose myself to it, even for a matter of seconds, my skin erupts and I am subjected to the most profound discomfort. I have therefore to live in this...' he gestured around the room, '...odd building, which has been designed to ensure that no natural light can ever penetrate. Fortunately electric light has no detrimental effect.' He indicated the overhead lamp that had been turned on as he entered the room.

'The bedside lamps didn't work,' Corinda said.

'I had them disconnected. I thought you needed rest.'

'So how did I get here?' she asked again, enjoying the coffee and finishing the first croissant.

He indicated one of the identical women. 'Iluska found you on the beach. You'd been washed ashore. You are very lucky to be alive.' He was looking at the way her breasts rose and fell with each breath she took.

'The yacht I was on... where's Tim? Did you find him too?'

Constantine shook his head. 'Sadly we found no one else. A little wreckage, nothing more.' The truth was they had found Corinda, unconscious, and Tim in a life-raft after they'd looted the sinking yacht. 'You must have been the sole survivor.'

Corinda put down the croissant. The news made her lose her appetite.

'You must eat,' Constantine admonished.

'He's dead then.'

'Not necessarily,' replied Constantine, who did not want to alarm or depress the girl. 'He's probably perfectly all right. There's a lot of shipping comes through these straits. I'm sure he got picked up.'

'Do you really think so? It was very stormy.'

'I'm sure of it. Please eat some more. You've got to keep your strength up.'

'Can we try and find him?'

'What was the name of your yacht?' Constantine asked, closely observing the subtle details of her beauty. Her legs were spectacular; long and slender and finely contoured. She was a prize indeed.

'I don't know. It belonged to my father.'

'We must get in touch with him then.'

'No, he's been dead for some years. I mean it belonged to his estate. Tim was one of the executors of his will,' explained Corinda.

'I see. Who should we contact then?' Constantine hadn't the slightest intention of contacting anyone but he wanted to put the girl at ease.

Corinda thought for a moment. She suddenly realised that not only could she not remember Tim's last name, or the firm for which he worked, but she hadn't the faintest idea of the official name of the island where she had been brought up. She didn't know Arabella's surname either. 'I don't know,' she said.

'There must be someone?'

'The solicitor's where Tim worked...'

'Yes?'

'I can't remember the name. It's the same as his I think.'

'You have been through a terrible experience, my dear. It is normal that the shock will have affected your memory. Just relax. It will all come back to you in time.' He got to his feet. 'Enjoy your breakfast. Rest. That's the bathroom.' He indicated the door in the corner of the room. 'You will dine with me tonight, please. By then I am sure you will have remembered everything.' He looked at her naked body with a proprietorial air. After all, it belonged to him now.

'I'm sorry, I really haven't thanked you. You saved my life.'

'Nonsense, my dear. I'm just delighted I was able to help. I'll see you at seven for dinner. Please rest.'

'I need some clothes,' Corinda said.

'Of course. I'll send my major-domo with everything you need.'

'You're being so kind.'

'Think nothing of it. There's one thing. These doors...' he gestured towards the doorway, 'I'm afraid they cannot be opened from the inside.' There were eight rooms like this for his prisoners. All had their own bathrooms. None had windows or any other means of escape. 'I have a fear of anyone letting in light by accident, you see. So if you want anything just press the button on the bedside table. Iluska or Irina will come at once.'

Corinda saw a small white button on the side of the bedside table. Though she thought it odd, she accepted his explanation without demur. She was too grateful to want to question his word.

'I'm feeling quite tired. I'll be fine.'

'Good. See you later then.'

The two girls walked out and Constantine followed. The metal shutter rolled down, ending its journey with a clang so loud it made Corinda start.

She finished her breakfast, eating another croissant and some fruit. She drank all the coffee and put both trays on the floor by the doorway before investigating the bathroom. It was tiled in blue with a white bathtub, wash-basin and toilet. There was a separate shower cubicle in frosted glass. After she'd used the toilet she took a long hot shower, the needles of water at first reviving her then making her feel terribly tired. As she turned it off and wrapped her body in one of the large white bath towels hanging from a heated rail, a wave of weariness washed over her. It was partly sadness too. She wouldn't be happy until she knew Tim was safe.

Without having the energy to dry herself, she walked back into the bedroom and sat on the bed. She was thinking about Arabella too. How long would it be before she realised the yacht had not reached its destination? Had the captain had time to radio a distress signal? Would she be out there on the sea now searching for her, worried sick for her safety?

Other thoughts crowded in on her. Who was this strange man who had rescued her and brought her to this even stranger house? What did he do? There were a lot of questions she wanted to ask him.

For the moment however, her body still needed rest. She lay on her side, curled into a ball and in a matter of seconds was fast asleep.

Chapter Four

For the second time the clanking of the metal shutter woke Corinda. This time her eyes needed no adjustment. The lights had been left on while she slept.

As she sat up, yawning and stretching, a tall woman strode confidently into the room. She had a strong, powerful body that rippled with muscles, and cropped black hair. Her skin was the colour of coffee.

'Have you been asleep?' she asked.

'Yes,' Corinda replied dozily.

'I'm Eloisa,' the woman said. She was dressed in a skin-tight tube of white Lycra that ran from just above her small breasts to the middle of her thighs. Her legs were sheathed in shiny black nylon, and she wore shoes with the highest heels Corinda had ever seen. Over her left arm she was carrying a selection of clothes. 'These are for you.' She dropped them on the bed. 'Constantine told me all about you. He was right; you are very beautiful.'

'Am I?' She remembered Tim telling her the same thing. She was starting to believe it.

'Of course you are. How are you feeling?'

'Better, I think. I'm very hungry again.'

'Good. Dinner's in an hour's time.' Eloisa was examining Corinda's body as inquisitively as Constantine had. Her eyes lingered lustfully on her neat triangle of blonde pubic hair. 'Would you like me to help you get ready?'

'Would you? I'm not very experienced with sophisticated clothes and suchlike.'

Eloisa knew that. Tim had told them everything about the girl's background. The information made Constantine very happy. His activities had never netted a virgin before. 'Let's go into the bathroom,' the woman said. 'There's make-up in there. Perhaps you'd like a bath first?'

Corinda got to her feet. 'Are you American?' There had been no television on the island, only a radio tuned to the World Service, which she had listened to avidly.

'Yes. But I've been away a long time.' She began running water into the bathtub.

'I don't suppose there's any news?' Corinda asked.

'News?'

'Any more survivors?'

'No, afraid not. This will relax you.' Eloisa poured sweet-smelling bath oil into the water.

'I'm so worried about my friend.'

'Sure you are. It's natural. But he'll be fine. Come on, get in and I'll do your back.'

Corinda climbed into the tub. Eloisa took a natural sponge and used it to soap the blonde's back. 'Oh, that's nice. Arabella always did that for me.'

'Who's Arabella?'

'My tutor. And my guardian, I suppose. She looked after me.'

'And she used to bathe you?'

'Only when I was a child. After that we took baths together.'

'Together? Sounds nice.' Eloisa hid her surprise. Perhaps the girl was not so innocent after all.

'Mmm...' Corinda remembered how Arabella had made her feel, the way her fingers had massaged and caressed, lathered her body, working the soap over her breasts and down between her legs. The memory made her nipples pucker, a fact that did not escape Eloisa.

'What sort of things did she do to you?'

'Oh, you know,' Corinda replied as if it were perfectly natural for two females to touch each other intimately, 'all those lovely sexy things.'

Eloisa did not need to be drawn a picture. 'What, like this?' she said, running the sponge down over Corinda's shoulder and onto her breasts, creating a thick lather. Then she used both hands to knead the pliant flesh.

'Oh yes, just like that. How did you know?'

'Because I like that too.'

'All women do, don't they?'

'Yes. And what about this?' Eloisa brought her hand up to Corinda's face, tilting it up so she could kiss her. She kissed her lightly at first, just grazing her lips, then crushed her mouth down powerfully and felt Corinda sucking her tongue. As their mouths squirmed together Eloisa pinched Corinda's hardened nipples.

'Oh yes...' Corinda purred, her lips still against the American's. Groping up she found the top of the white dress and tugged it down, freeing her small firm breasts. She massaged them both with the same hand. They felt entirely different from Arabella's; not soft and resilient, but sinewy and inflexible, though the nipples were no less sensitive and Eloisa shuddered as Corinda pinched them.

'That's good,' Eloisa gasped, breaking the kiss. It was a new experience for her. Most of the girls who arrived on the island, and who were passed on to her as crumbs from her master's table, had little experience of lesbian love and had to be persuaded that it was in their best interest to cooperate with her desires. Corinda not only had no such inhibitions, but appeared to want to take the lead.

With her lips free Corinda fastened them to Eloisa's breasts. She sucked her left nipple, and then the right, nipping them between her teeth then flicking them with her tongue.

'Kiss my breasts now; I love that,' Corinda said, splashing them with water to wash away the soap then presenting them to the American by sitting up straight.

Eloisa did not need to be asked twice. With her own breasts hanging out of the front of her dress she leant forward and sucked Corinda's nearest nipple into her mouth. She pinched it forcibly with her teeth and heard Corinda moan.

'We used to use the soap,' Corinda whispered, as though it were a secret. In a way it was. She had never told anyone else. There had never been anyone else to tell.

Without relinquishing her mouth's grip on Corinda's nipple, Eloisa groped around for the bar of soap. She found it and pushed it down into the water as Corinda spread her legs as far apart as the sides of the bathtub would allow. Eloisa pressed the edge of the soap into her labia, just as Arabella had done so many times. Corinda sighed with delight as she felt the soap sliding up and down against her clitoris.

'Oh, if makes me feel so good.'

'Will you come for me?' Eloisa asked, to test how far the girl would go. She was looking straight into Corinda's big blue eyes.

'Oh, can I? Will you let me?' Corinda closed her eyes and let the pleasure wash over her, feeling confused. As the soap produced spasms of sexual sensation she thought of Arabella. This woman was completely different, and yet essentially the same. Where Arabella's body had been soft and melting, this woman was hard and muscular. But the way she made her feel, the beautifully delicate way she rubbed the smooth soap against exactly the right spot was the same. It provoked the same needs and created the means to satisfy them. She felt her body churning. Suddenly she thought of Tim. She saw herself astride his hips with his penis nosing into her sex. She remembered how hot it had been and how it pulsed.

Eloisa adjusted the rhythm of her stroke, matching it to the little undulations of Corinda's body. 'Come for me,' she whispered.

'Yes, yes.' Corinda arched her back, pushing her pelvis up out of the water, as the last movement of the soap catapulted her into an orgasm.

Eloisa felt her own body pulse as she watched the girl stretched out on a rack of pleasure, the water dripping from her breasts.

Slowly the moment passed. Corinda lowered herself back into the water. 'Oh, that was so good,' she said. 'I feel great.' It was true. The aftermath of a delicious orgasm seemed to have washed away her worries. She felt optimistic. Tim would be safe. They would find a way of contacting Arabella. Everything was going to be all right. She felt no embarrassment. To her what had happened had been the most natural thing in the world.

She stood up. The water cascaded off her body. Arabella had always been very strict about one thing. Favours had to be returned.

Eloisa had sunk to her knees at the side of the bath. Corinda climbed out, wrapped a towel around her body then took Eloisa's hand and drew her to her feet. She kissed her. Eloisa had definitely not anticipated this. She had come to do Constantine's bidding, to prepare the girl for him. She hadn't imagined this would happen. Tim had said nothing about the girl's lesbian experience and Eloisa suspected that was because he didn't know about it.

Corinda's hand pulled the American's dress up at the back and delved down between her buttocks. Eloisa was not wearing panties and the sleek black nylons were hold-ups. There was nothing to stop Corinda's fingers slipping between her labia then forcing their way into her vagina. 'Like this?' she asked.

'No, like this,' the American replied. There were so many things she would have loved to do with the girl, like take her to her room, string her up to the wall and use a whip on her. She would have loved to strap on a dildo and take her from behind. But Constantine would be annoyed if she scared her. He wanted her innocence intact. Instead Eloisa twisted out of the girl's arms, gripped the edge of the bath and bent over until her back was straight and at right angles to her legs. She wormed her feet, still in the high-heeled shoes, wide apart. 'Did you lick it for your Arabella?' she asked.

By way of reply Corinda dropped to her knees. She wrapped her arms around Eloisa's strong thighs and manoeuvred her head back, until her eyes were staring up at the woman's shaven pubis, and her mouth was immediately below her sex. She pushed her tongue between the labia and licked all the way from the bud of her anus to her clit. Then she worked back again, pushing against her sphincter. It gave way and Corinda plunged her tongue inside, trying to penetrate as deeply as she could. Smoothing over the welts of the hold-up stockings, which clung tightly to her thighs, she insinuated the fingertips of her right hand into the woman's vagina, penetrating her there too.

'God, you're good,' Eloisa sighed as she felt her sex producing a wave of juice.

Corinda moved her fingers out of the way, allowing her mouth to replace them, circling her tongue around the entrance to her vagina, stretching the elastic flesh this way and that before plunging inside. She licked at the wetness, enjoying the taste, pushing her face against the American's sex to get her tongue deeper. She darted it in and out, as Arabella had taught her to do. She found Eloisa's clitoris and licked it, two fingers in her vagina and two in her anus.

Eloisa's body tightened. Her knuckles whitened as she gripped the edge of the bath. Normally her sexuality was more complicated, more perverse, and needed the stimulus of total domination, but there was something about this girl that excited her as much as the whips and bondage that were the usual familiars to her passion. It was, she supposed, the girl's essential innocence and her readiness to please. These were traits that seemed at odds with her sexual proficiency.

She found herself sobbing as her head reared up and a jolt of pleasure coursed through her. 'You're so good,' she managed to say through clenched teeth. And it was true. The blonde's fingers seemed to have wormed their way deeper than she'd thought fingers could ever go. They burrowed into her as copious juices ran down them, and her sex spasmed rhythmically. But the pleasure from her clitoris was just as acute. The girl's tongue was barely moving but it had found the perfect spot, a raw nerve that was creating wave after wave of pure sexual ecstasy. The two-pronged assault on her senses began to merge. She could no longer tell which was producing the greater pleasure. Was it the delicate movement of Corinda's tongue, or the fingers pumping into her vagina and anus, that finally broke the dam of feelings and plunged her into an orgasm? She did not know or care. Her body went rigid, and she heard herself let out a strange sound, like a cross between a scream and a moan. It echoed around the bathroom, only seeming to die away as the throes of orgasm died away too.

Corinda rocked back on her haunches as Eloisa straightened up.

'You're something,' she said.

'Was it good?' Corinda asked.

Eloisa smiled. 'You know it was. Come on. We've got to get you ready. Can't keep Constantine Evangelos Stephanikis waiting. She pulled the tight white Lycra down over her thighs, and back up around her bosom.

There was a black silk bra, matching panties and a suspender belt, all trimmed with lace. The tight cocktail dress was a scarlet red, and there were shiny red high heels in almost exactly the same colour. Eloisa had plenty of clothes to choose from. There were wardrobes of clothes all salvaged from shipwrecked yachts. As the yachts had usually been the property of very rich men the clothes were expensive too, with all the top couturiers represented among Constantine's looted treasures.

Eloisa's hand was still trembling slightly as she helped Corinda wash and dry her long blonde hair. That done, she sat her on a small stool and applied a little make-up. The girl didn't need much; a touch of eyeliner and shadow to emphasis her eyes, a little blusher to accentuate her cheekbones, and red lipstick to coat her pouting lips.

'This is beautiful,' Corinda said, picking up the dress as they walked back into the bedroom. 'And these.' She picked up the lingerie. They reminded her of the underwear she had worn on the yacht. She rubbed the panties against her face. 'It's so soft.'

'Silk,' Eloisa said.

'What's this?' Corinda held up the suspender belt.

'Haven't you seen one before?'

'No.'

'It's for holding up stockings.'

'Stockings?'

'Like these.' Eloisa indicated her own legs.

'But they stay up on their own.'

'Some do. Some don't. These don't.' She picked up the cellophane packet of black stockings that also lay on the bed.

'I've only ever seen tights. Sometimes when it was cold on the island I'd wear tights.'

'You've never worn stockings?'

'Never.'

Eloisa took the suspender belt and wrapped it around Corinda's waist, clipping it in place at the small of her back. Its suspenders, like long fingers, reached down the front and side of her thighs. Eloisa undid the packet of stockings and shook them out. They were the sheerest black.

'Sit on the bed,' she said.

Corinda obeyed. The American worked one of the stockings into a neat pocket and handed it to Corinda. Raising her foot the blonde dug her toes into the nylon then rolled it up her leg, watching with fascination as the shiny tight material seemed to transform her flesh, leaving it sheer and wet-looking, like a coat of gloss paint. She smoothed the top onto her thigh. The contrast between it and the flesh above it was marked. Above the nylon her tanned skin seemed impossibly soft.

'Sexy, isn't it?' Eloisa said, spotting Corinda's reaction. 'That's why men love women to wear stockings.'

'The thing is, I haven't had much experience with men,' Corinda said, as she picked up the second stocking and gathered the nylon into a pocket around the toe, as she'd seen Eloisa do with the first.

'Take it from me,' Eloisa assured her.

As she rolled the stocking up her leg she thought it odd that Eloisa had not asked her a single question about her background or her life; perhaps Constantine had told her not to, fearing perhaps such questions might upset her.

With both welts smoothed tightly around her thighs she felt a twinge of excitement as she looked down at them.

'Like this,' Eloisa said, showing her how the rubber nub of the suspender slid under the nylon and was then secured into the metal hoop on top of it.

43

Corinda tried the second one for herself. By the time she had clipped the fourth into place she could accomplish the manoeuvre without difficulty.

She jumped to her feet. The suspender belt felt strange. She had never worn anything like it. The way it pulled at the stockings, keeping them taut against her flesh, made her feel curiously aroused. She was also excited by the way her sex felt open and exposed, as though the suspender belt had been designed to frame and display it.

'Makes me feel sexy,' she said.

'That's good, isn't it? Clothes can do that. There's all sorts of stuff you can wear that'll get you turned on. I like really tight things; basques and bustiers, especially in leather. Constantine's going to get a wardrobe moved in here while you're having dinner. I'll have it stocked up with a load of lingerie, as well as dresses. I think I guessed your size right.'

'Does Constantine like stockings?' Corinda stroked the nylon.

'Sure he does. Crazy about them.'

'Good. I want to please him. He's been so kind.' The sexual excitement Corinda felt increased markedly when she thought of him. The experience in the bathroom had only been, she hoped, a prelude to the main event. Though she could not say that she felt the same about him as she had felt about Tim, in terms of finding him handsome and attractive, he was nevertheless only the second man she had met and been close to. She hoped over dinner she would be able to persuade him to let her see his body, as she had persuaded Tim. She would quite understand if he didn't want to have sex with her, but it would be nice if he would at least agree to let her see him and perhaps touch him. Of course, if she could persuade him to go further that would be even better. After having been so near on the yacht to feeling a real live penis sinking into her, it was an experience she now craved. It would be wonderful if Constantine was in the mood to allow her to at least satisfy her curiosity.

Of course, she reminded herself, she was his guest and she had a lot to thank him for. If he did not want to have sex with her she must not show her disappointment; that would be rude after everything he'd done. But she didn't think it would hurt to ask at least.

Clipping the black bra into place she looked at Eloisa as she picked up the panties. 'Can I ask you a personal question?'

'Sure.'

'Do I have to wear these? I feel so much better without them.'

Eloisa smiled. 'You do whatever you want, sister.'

Corinda dropped the panties on the bed. She picked up the red dress and stepped into it. As Eloisa zipped her up the dress wrapped around her, encasing her tightly. The low neckline revealed the deep cleavage created by the bra, while the rest of the dress clung to the contours of her hourglass figure. It followed her narrow waist, the dramatic flare of her hips, and sheathed the pert curves of her buttocks.

'Well?' She danced into the bathroom and inspected herself in the long mirror fixed to the inside of the door.

'You look great,' Eloisa said. 'It's time to go. Don't want to keep him waiting.'

Corinda walked to the bed, placed the shoes on the floor and slipped her feet into them. 'I've only worn heels once before. I'm a bit wonky on them.'

Again she found it a little odd that Eloisa didn't ask her why but said, instead, 'Don't worry, I'll walk real slow. Let's go.'

Somehow the metal shutter, which had closed the moment Eloisa entered the room, began to roll up. It was the first time Corinda had stepped outside the room. She found herself in a corridor with plain white walls and a black tiled floor. There were similar metal-shuttered doorways on either side. The corridor opened on to a large square atrium with a white marble floor. A long wooden staircase ran along one wall, its steps made from trunks of trees sawn into short lengths and only planed flat on the upper surface. The logs were jointed into a massive tree trunk which ran diagonally up to a gallery.

At first Corinda thought the ceiling of the atrium was made from glass and that above it she could see the sky, dotted with stars and a crescent moon. It was only when she looked closely that she realised it was a cleverly created illusion, the moon and stars painted on a background above a glass screen.

Eloisa led the way across the atrium into a large reception room. At the far end was a huge fireplace, its tapering chimney standing out from the wall. A roaring fire blazed in the grate. Two vast white brocade sofas were positioned in front of it, with a polished oak coffee table between them. The table was piled with books, all on the works of twentieth-century artists. There were more books on thick plate-glass shelves cantilevered out from one wall, and the whole room was dotted with beautifully made wooden stands on the tops of which were displayed various antiquities; a Roman head, an Egyptian jug, an Etruscan bowl. Each was individually lit by a spotlight set into the ceiling directly above.

Constantine Evangelos Stephanikis stood by the fire. He was wearing a white dinner jacket, black trousers, a black bow tie, and a silk cummerbund in red and blue.

'My dear, you look charming, totally charming,' he said as Corinda walked, a little unsteadily, across the room.

'Thank you,' she said.

He took her hand and kissed it, before holding her arm up to inspect her more closely.

'Champagne? A glass before dinner? Eloisa...' There was a bottle in a silver ice bucket on the coffee table. Eloisa poured some into two crystal flutes, and handed them to him and Corinda.

'You may leave us now,' he said.

'Enjoy,' Eloisa responded enigmatically, looking directly at him, then turned and left.

'So here is to you, my dear. Saved from the sea.' He raised his glass and clinked it against Corinda's.

'And to you, for saving me.' She sipped her drink.

Constantine laughed. 'No, I cannot take credit for that. I merely found you. A higher fate, I think, was responsible for throwing you up on my island. Shall we call it destiny? Are you hungry?'

'I'm starving,' she replied.

'My chef is Greek, like myself, but he will prepare you anything you wish if you do not care for Greek food.'

'No, I love it.'

'Good, good, then let us delay no longer. Bring the champagne with you.'

Constantine took her arm. There was an archway to one side of the fireplace and he led her through it into a dining room with an elaborately carved oak table that could have seated at least thirty people. One end had been set for two people, with a sparkling array of crystal glasses, silver candlesticks, gold-rimmed white china and solid silver cutlery laid on crisp white linen.

There was a French window along one wall, giving the impression the room looked out on to a lush tropical garden. In fact it was another illusion; a three-dimensional trompe l'oeil. The painting was arranged on a three-sided screen outside the glass.

Constantine followed Corinda's eyes. 'Yes, it's a fake. I like to pretend. It is very clever. A computer controls the background light. As dawn breaks outside so the whole picture changes to a bright blue sky.'

'Really?'

'At least I have an illusion of reality. Please,' he said, pulling out one of the dining chairs, just as the waiter had done on the yacht.

Corinda sat, and he sat opposite her. There was a small gold bell on the table, which he rang. He lifted his champagne glass and touched it against Corinda's again. 'To a wonderful evening.'

'You're so kind.'

Her reaction to the Greek was complicated. She didn't find him in the least attractive, but that had not, apparently, stopped her body tingling with an anticipation that was unmistakably sexual. Perhaps this was what she had read about; the chemical reaction women feel when with a man.

A door opened and one of the brunettes who had accompanied Constantine earlier entered. She was dressed in a tight leotard made from transparent plastic. Her full breasts, nipples and neatly trimmed pubic hair were exposed. She wore high-heeled boots of white leather.

'Iluska, we're ready to eat. My guest is happy to join me with the Greek food.'

Iluska nodded and went back through the door. Having little experience of what was considered normal, and what was not, Corinda did not think the brunette's outfit at all strange. She did think she was extremely beautiful though, and compared herself unfavourably with Iluska's dark good looks. If Constantine was surrounded by women like Iluska, she thought, it was unlikely he would need sex with her.

'Have you remembered anything yet, my dear?' he asked. He had spent all day

46

on the phone to his contacts telling them of his unusual piece of merchandise. There was no doubt Corinda would fetch a good price on the market he dealt with. A very good price.

'I'm afraid I fell asleep again,' she explained.

'Never mind. It will come in time. Better not to force these things.'

The door opened and Iluska came out followed by the other brunette, who was dressed in an identical costume. The two carried trays of food and set down little pottery bowls on the table, in the traditional Greek meze. There was hummus, tabouleh, taramasalata, tzatziki, and dolmades, all dressed with olive oil and mint. There were clams, huge prawns, three different types of oysters and a basket of breads; pitta bread and a flat focaccia, baked with black olives.

Corinda ate voraciously, tearing off chunks of bread to dip into the bowls, while one of the two lewdly dressed women poured a heady red wine into her glass. Constantine ate with relish too, consuming oysters first, before turning to the prawns. He shelled them expertly, then sucked their heads before consuming their tails.

The initial hunger was eventually, at least partly satiated. By the time the girls cleared away the first course and brought plates of charcoal grilled lamb, quails and chicken, Corinda felt able to pause long enough to ask some of the questions she had been storing up.

'Where exactly are we, Mr Stephanikis?'

'Oh, please, you must call me Constantine. We are on an island to the north of Cyprus. Apart from this house, it is uninhabited.'

'And how long have you lived here?'

He shrugged. 'My unfortunate condition makes it necessary to live in absolute isolation. Originally I lived in Athens but it was impossible to guarantee that I was not exposed, accidentally, to sunlight. Fortunately I had sufficient resources to buy this island, and constructed this specially designed house. Otherwise my life would have been impossible.'

'Is there no cure?'

'The condition is extremely rare. Perhaps if it were not more doctors would take an interest. As it is there appears to be no hope.'

'I'm so sorry.' Corinda's heart went out to the man.

Constantine took a grilled quail in his fingers and tore it apart. He fed the pieces into his mouth and crunched on the bones. 'Don't be. I enjoy life. I am surrounded by beautiful things and,' he gestured to one of the brunettes who stood by attentively should anything be needed, 'beautiful women. I am a very lucky man. The absence of sunlight is a small price to pay.'

'But the fresh air?'

'I go out at night. I see the stars and the moon. I smell the sea. It is enough.'

Corinda bit into a piece of grilled lamb. It was tender and moist but she suddenly felt full. 'I don't think I can eat any more.'

'Some fruit then?'

'A little perhaps.'

'Irina,' he said, turning to the brunette, then spoke a few words in a language Corinda did not understand. The girl immediately began to clear the table. She was joined by Iluska. 'They are Albanian,' Constantine explained. 'Iluska has learned a little English but Irina speaks only Albanian. Life in that blighted country is so wretched they find conditions here infinitely preferable. They used to work for a man who kept them shackled like slaves.'

'Really?' Corinda was astonished.

'So I suppose you could say I rescued them too.' It was something like the truth. The girls had been rescued by Constantine in the sense that he had fished them from the water after having been responsible for sinking the boat on which they had stowed away in an effort to escape the deprivations of their mother country. But they had never been anyone's slaves. Not until now, at least. Constantine had taken such a fancy to them he decided not to sell them on, as he normally did with attractive women, but to keep them for himself. Their life in Tirane had been so appalling that serving Constantine's every whim and, occasionally, having to suffer Eloisa's unwanted attentions, was luxurious by comparison. He had kept them chained at night, until he convinced them that conditions in the rest of the world were as bad as in Albania and they would never find a better life.

A large platter of fruit consisting of pawpaw, kiwi, mango, water melon, strawberries and grapes, all seeded and peeled, was set on the table together with a white bowl of yogurt and another of thin honey. Irina brought two steaming cups of muddy Turkish coffee.

'How do you get all this food if there's no one else on the island?'

'A boat comes twice a week. We have every convenience. And, of course, my men catch fish.'

'Mr Step... I mean, Constantine. Can I ask you something? Will you give me an honest answer?'

'Of course, my dear. What is troubling you?'

'It's just that... I don't know how to begin. I've lived a very sheltered life. My mother... I've only just found out about this; apparently two men did terrible things to her. My father decided he wanted to keep me away from men. Well, you see what I'm trying to say is that I have no experience. I mean, you're only the second man I've ever even met.'

'That is quite extraordinary,' Constantine said, trying to sound surprised. He was glad to hear the young man had told him the truth.

'So you see, it's very difficult for me.'

'What was your question?'

'I wondered... I just wanted to know if you find me attractive?'

Constantine laughed, a shrill, high-pitched sound. 'My dear, you must take it from me, you are an extremely beautiful young woman.'

'Really?' She was pleased.

'And I can assure you, I am a connoisseur in such matters.'

'You find me attractive?'

'Any man of passion would find you quite delectable.'

'Well then, if that is the case...' she faltered.

'Yes?'

'This is more difficult to say. I don't want you to be offended. Especially after everything you've done for me.'

'I promise you, my dear girl, I will not be.'

'It's just that... well, just before the shipwreck...' She wasn't sure how to phrase what she wanted to say. 'I was naturally curious, you see. I was asking Tim; you remember, the man I was with? I was asking him if I could see his body, because I'd never seen a man before.'

'Is that so?'

'Never.'

'And how did he react?'

'He was so nice, Constantine. He let me have a really good look. He even got engorged for me. That's the right word, isn't it? You know, when a man gets sexually excited. Well, that was just a few minutes before the boat was hit.'

'I see.'

'So I was wondering... I mean, I know it's a lot to ask, and perhaps I should wait for a day or so, but I just wondered if you'd do the same. Show me your body, I mean. And...'

'And?'

'You can always say no, if it's asking too much.'

'What?'

'Well, I wondered if, at the same time, you might have sex with me. Just for a little while. It wouldn't take long.'

'You've never had sex before?'

'Not with a man. I've had plenty of sex with a woman though, so I'm sure I wouldn't be too bad at it. My tutor taught me a lot.'

'Did she?' Constantine raised an eyebrow. This was news to him, but interesting news. 'And did you enjoy it?'

'Oh yes, very much. But it's not the same as with a man, is it?'

'No, I don't imagine it is.'

'Will you help me, Constantine? Please?'

'My dear girl, I will do anything you ask. How could any man refuse you?'

Corinda danced to her feet, came round the table, threw her arms around his neck and kissed him on the cheek. 'Oh Constantine, that's so wonderful. And look...' She stood back and wriggled the tight red skirt of the dress up over her hips until he could see her thighs sheathed in sheer stockings. 'Eloisa said you would like these.'

'I do. They suit you.'

'They make me feel very sexy, I think. I've never worn stockings before. Should I have worn panties?' She pulled the skirt up a little further to reveal her pubes. 'I got so used to running around without anything on.'

'I like you like this.' The girl's pubic hair was thin enough for him to be able

49

to see the crease of her sex. 'Sit up here on the table,' he said, pushing away his coffee cup and pulling his chair back.

Corinda levered herself up onto the table's edge, her skirt still around her hips. 'Here?'

'Yes.' He put a hand on her thighs, his palm resting on one of the suspenders. 'There is one thing, Corinda.'

'Yes?'

'You must do whatever I ask of you, without question.'

'Of course I will,' she said earnestly, staring into his pink eyes. Her excitement and enthusiasm seemed to have changed her perception of him. At that moment she could not think of him as anything but handsome. The bullfrog had turned into prince charming.

Irina still stood silently by. Constantine fired a number of words at her and she immediately began to clear the table.

'Do you find Irina attractive?' he asked.

'Oh yes, she's gorgeous.'

'You would like to have sex with her?'

'I'd like to have sex with both of them. They look like sisters.'

'But they are not,' Constantine said.

Iluska had joined her companion to help ferry things to the kitchen.

Constantine's hand stroked Corinda's thigh. 'Now what was it you wanted to see?'

'Could we start with your penis?' she asked. 'Is it hard?'

'A little.'

'Oh good. Tim's was hard when I first saw it, so I didn't see it grow.'

Constantine stood up. He took off his jacket and unclipped his cummerbund. 'Irina,' he said, handing her the clothes. He spoke in rapid Albanian again, and Iluska moved in front of him, loosening his bow tie and unbuttoning his shirt. Irina eased off his shoes and socks as he held his feet up one at a time. Iluska removed his shirt and unzipped the fly of his trousers. She skinned them down with his black briefs and he stepped out of them, leaving himself naked.

'Is this what you wanted?' he asked.

Corinda stared at his body. It was quite different from Tim's. Not only was he covered in a mat of white hair, his arms and legs were far bigger and his belly round, like a cushion of flesh. His penis was small, and from what she could see it was more veined and gnarled than Tim's.

The two brunettes had finished clearing the table. They folded Constantine's clothes neatly over one of the dining chairs and left the room.

'Are you going to make it grow now?' Corinda asked.

'Open your legs a little and watch it closely. You'll see it grow.'

As Corinda eased her legs apart Constantine feasted his eyes on the delicate lips of her sex.

'Yes, look at that,' Corinda said. Without thinking she squirmed off the table and dropped to her knees in front of him to get a close look.

'Put a fingertip here,' he said, pointing at the ridge at the base of his circumcised glans.

Corinda did as she was told. Almost the moment she touched it she saw it expand, the veins pumping visibly. It grew rapidly. 'My, look at that! Just touching makes that happen?'

'All sorts of things make that happen,' he told her.

'Really?'

'I think you should take your dress off.'

'But I want it to stay hard.'

'It will. Looking at your body will keep it hard.'

Without getting to her feet Corinda unzipped the dress and pulled it over her head. She shook out her long blonde hair so it cascaded over her shoulders. 'Would you mind if I took my bra off too? I'm not used to this type. They cut into me.'

'Take it off.'

Corinda unclipped the bra and pulled the shoulder straps down her arms. She leant forward and shook it off, her breasts quivering at their sudden freedom, her nipples already hard. She saw Constantine's cock twitch. 'Was that because of looking at me?'

'Yes. I told you, you're a very beautiful girl.'

She was naked now apart from the suspender belt and the sheer black stockings. 'Can I touch it again?'

'Of course.'

Corinda wrapped her hand around the fully erect shaft. It was not as long as Tim's, but it was much broader. She remembered her surprise at how hot it had been to the touch, and this one too seemed to radiate heat.

'What should I do now?' she asked.

He smiled. 'You are anxious to learn, aren't you?'

'Are you going to fuck me?' Arabella would have been shocked that she knew that word, but among the literary masterpieces she'd read on the island one of her tutors had brought her the works of James Joyce.

'My, my, and I thought you were an innocent.'

'Is that a bad thing to say?'

'No, it is quite charming. But first, I think, there is something else I should teach you. When you are with a woman, when you are having sex with a woman, do you use your mouth on her?'

'Of course.'

'Well then. You will see it is quite logical to do the same with a man.'

'Oh I know about that,' she said, pleased not to appear totally naive.

'Do you?'

'Do you like that better than fucking?'

'No, but some men do.'

'It makes them ejaculate, right?'

'Yes.'

51

'Can I do that to you? Will you let me? Just as an experiment.'

'Of course, my dear. I'm going to let you do whatever you want.'

Corinda leant forward. Tentatively she touched the tip of her tongue against the tip of Constantine's cock. Then she ran it around the pronounced rim at the base of the glans. This made his penis jerk and swell, so she repeated it, with the same result. She made a mental note of the effect, wanting to make sure she remembered it for future reference.

'Take it in your mouth,' Constantine said, his normally reedy voice thickened by excitement.

Corinda opened her mouth and slipped the glans between her lips. It stretched them wide. She sucked and felt it throb.

'Deeper. Take it deeper.'

A hand caressed her long blonde hair, then pressed. Corinda felt a frisson of alarm as his cock slid into her throat. At first she thought she was going to gag but she managed to control that reflex, and felt a strong surge of excitement. There seemed to be a direct connection between her mouth and her sex. It was almost as though his cock was jammed into her vagina. It was this that made her realise what she had to do. The reason men obviously liked this experience was that the mouth was a substitute for the vagina. Though she had never had a penis inside her she knew a man would push in and out, so it seemed clear she should try to imitate that movement if she was going to give Constantine the maximum pleasure.

She pulled back until his glans was at her lips, then drove forward, plunging his cock down deep into her throat. Repeating the process she sucked hard as she pulled back and heard him moan. She made another mental note.

'You learn fast,' he said.

Her head bobbed down, then up, her cheeks dimpled as she sucked. Constantine moaned again and she felt proud. She was a woman now, doing what a woman does to a man. She wanted to please him, to do something for him after everything he had done for her. She began to move with a rhythm, sliding her mouth up and down, taking him deeper and deeper in her throat and sucking harder.

Constantine looked down at her. Her hair streamed down over her naked back, her breasts trembling as she moved. He had debated all day whether he should take her virginity. Some of his customers would pay considerably more for her in a virgin state. But, he had told himself, money wasn't everything. The price he would get for a girl of such beauty would be quite high enough. And she would still have an essential innocence to add icing to the cake and increase the bidding. Life had handed him a unique opportunity and he decided to enjoy it.

He took her head in his hands to stay her movement, and pulled out of her mouth.

'What's the matter? Aren't I doing it right?' Corinda's face was creased with worry. 'I was getting carried away, wasn't I?'

'You were doing wonderfully, my dear.'

'Why haven't you ejaculated then? I wanted you to ejaculate. You said you would.'

'I said some men do. But I thought you wanted more.'

'I wanted to do whatever pleases you,' she said earnestly.

'Then we must go on to the next lesson.'

Corinda felt a sharp stab of excitement. Her sex was already wet and her nipples as hard as stone. 'You're going to put it inside me, aren't you?'

'Yes.'

'Oh Constantine, that's so nice of you. I'm so grateful.'

'I will enjoy it too.'

'What have I got to do?'

'Lie back on the table,' he said.

Corinda got to her feet. She was still wearing the high heels and her legs looked lithe and slender, the stockings making them look even longer than they were. 'Shall I keep the stockings on?'

'Oh yes.'

'You like them, don't you?' Corinda felt coquettish. She was beginning to realise that the hardness of Constantine's penis was directly related to the things she did and the way she looked. One of the stockings had wrinkled at the knee and she bent to smooth it out, stretching the nylon with her palms until it fitted like a second skin again. She straightened up as she adjusted the suspender to hold the stocking taut, and saw Constantine gazing at her legs.

'Arabella used to like to watch too,' she said.

'Who's Arabella?'

'My tutor. She used to like to watch me play with myself. It excited her. Would that excite you?' She ran one hand down between her legs. A finger slipped between her labia. Her clitoris was swollen with expectation. As her finger probed she gasped. She had never felt it so tender.

She hauled herself up onto the edge of the table again and opened her legs wider, allowing her hand more freedom of movement. She kicked off the shoes and brought her feet up to the table-top, so her legs were bent and Constantine could see her sex. Her hand parted her labia, and she penetrated her vagina with two fingers.

'Do you like that?' she asked.

'Lie back,' he said.

Corinda obeyed. The polished oak was cold against her back. Constantine moved in front of her, staring down at her sex. He took her wrist and pulled her hand away, drawing her towards him slightly, then he pulled her legs around his waist, her buttocks suspended over the edge of the table, her vagina no more than an inch from his cock. The nylon rasped against his flesh. He fingered her thighs, feeling the difference between the nylon and her soft flesh. With her legs spread her labia had opened and he could see the pink nodule of her clitoris. It was glistening wet.

Slowly he moved, until his erection nudged into her sex.

'Oh, Constantine,' she panted, 'I'm so excited. I can feel your penis. Are you going to do it to me now?' She raised her head to watch.

'Yes,' he said gruffly, no longer concerned with her needs. His fingers dug into her thighs and he pulled her onto him, the tip of his glans sliding into the tight channel of her labia, until it fitted neatly to the entrance of her vagina. His penis throbbed and his balls ached. She was his, this was his prize. He could see the soft wet flesh of her sex pursed around his glans as though welcoming it with a kiss.

The time for finesse had passed. He plunged, driving his cock into the depths of a vagina, where he knew no man had been before.

'God! Oh God!' Corinda screamed. She could not hold her head up and dropped back onto the table. How many times had she imagined what it would feel like to have a man inside her? And now it was done, her sex filled with hot, hard, living flesh. The shock of sensation of the initial lunge was almost strong enough to make her orgasm instantly. Constantine did not begin a rhythm, sawing in and out of her as she'd expected him to. Instead he ground forward, pulling her onto him, rocking from side to side, grinding the base of his cock against her clitoris, trying with all his strength to get deeper.

'Oh God,' she screamed, the sensations already erupting from the depths of her, suddenly joined by the feelings from her clit. Her orgasm exploded, like the white light of a flashbulb, quick and intense. But instead of her body relaxing she found no release at all, the first orgasm only a prelude to the second.

She felt different now, more confident. She wriggled down on the rigid flesh stuffed inside her.

'It's wonderful, wonderful,' she rambled.

He grunted, in no mood for her girlish enthusiasm, wanting only his own satisfaction.

'Turn over,' he said.

He would have liked to bugger her, to take his bone-hard cock and push it into her smaller orifice, which he was sure had never been used either. But his excitement was too intense. He could hold out long enough for one more manoeuvre and that was all. He pulled out of her, his cock soaked with her copious fluid, and twisted her round onto her stomach.

'On your knees,' he said.

She obeyed, getting onto all fours on the polished oak. He crawled up onto the table behind her, grabbed her hips and the black suspender belt and plunged into the slickness of her sex again.

'Oh yes!' she cried, feeling a whole set of new sensations as his cock explored the new angles this position offered. 'Are you going to come? Are you?'

She came again, the words provoking her as much as the physical sensation, the image of his cock ejaculating in the depths of her body making her second orgasm more shattering than the first. Desperately she fought to get herself back under control. This was the first time she had ever been fucked, and she was determined not to miss his ejaculation. Despite her inexperience she knew Constantine was close to that moment. She seemed to be able to feel his semen, pumping up into his cock. She could feel it jerking against the silky wet confines of her sex. He was thrusting in and out, withdrawing almost all the way before plunging back in again.

It felt so good, so real, so adult. She was a woman now. A proper woman. Her body was reacting of its own accord. She could feel her vagina contracting, each thrust of his cock opening it for him, allowing him deeper.

She was coming again but she fought it, trying to hold it off until she felt him come.

'This is what you wanted, isn't it?' he said between gritted teeth.

'Yes. Oh yes.'

She twisted her head around to look at him. Constantine's big body was rigid, his muscles hard, sweat running down his face, the effort turning his chalky complexion a bright pink. His eyes were locked on her buttocks, watching as his cock drove between them.

Suddenly he stopped thrusting. He pulled her onto him with all his strength, and at that moment Corinda felt his cock spasm violently. Deep inside her she felt a hot wetness lashing against the tight tube of her sex as his phallus convulsed. She could not fight off her own climax any longer. What barriers she had managed to erect against her third orgasm simply crumbled away. She found herself shuddering and trembling and sobbing as it took hold of her body, like the hand of a giant, and wrung her out until every nerve was exhausted, every emotion spent.

'Oh, Constantine,' she gasped as soon as she recovered. 'Thank you, thank you. You've been so good to me. Will you do it again? Can we do it again?'

He pulled out of her. A large dollop of spunk dripped onto the table. 'Of course. But now you must rest.'

'When? When can we do it again? Tomorrow?'

'Yes, tomorrow.'

'Promise? Do you promise me?'

'Of course, my dear. I promise.'

Corinda was convinced that Constantine was the most wonderful man in the world.

Chapter Five

Constantine was a man of his word.

The metal shutter rolled up for the first time in the morning. An older woman in a black dress, with a white collar and cuffs, had delivered breakfast. The same woman returned with a light lunch, but clearly spoke no English as she answered Corinda's questions, as to whether she might go for a walk, with a shrug of her shoulders. The metal shutter rolled down for a second time as soon as the woman had gone, leaving Corinda alone once more, and though she did not see it that way, a prisoner.

When she got back to the room the previous night she found a walnut wardrobe had been added to the furniture. She was too tired to examine it then, but in the morning spent a lot of time sorting through the clothes it contained. They were all, without exception, expensive and beautiful creations in silk, satin, and chiffon. There was a drawer of lingerie too, and a rack of shoes in a variety of colours. She used the mirror in the bathroom, trying to decide what she would wear for Constantine that night.

Later she tried to read. The bookcase contained mainly classics she'd read before, but there were a few she had not; she picked a Dickens. But she found it hard to concentrate. Her mind kept replaying images of last night, her body prone to little tremors of delight as she remembered what had happened. Her sex was permanently wet, her clitoris constantly restless, her nipples hard.

She must have dozed off because the next thing she knew the electric motors of the metal shutter rolling up made her wake with a start.

'Constantine,' she said as the Greek strolled in. She jumped off the bed and kissed him on both cheeks. 'Oh, it's so good to see you.'

'And you, my dear. I'm sorry I have been so inattentive, but I fear I have been rather busy. So many things to do.' He was dressed in a white shirt and dark slacks again.

'As long as you're here now.'

'I have arranged a little treat for you.'

'A treat?'

'Here.' He had a white satin robe on his arm. He handed it to her. 'Put this on. We're going upstairs.'

Corinda wrapped the robe around her naked body. The material felt cold, but as the room was warm, like everywhere she had been in the house, it was a pleasant sensation. Normally the chill would have puckered her nipples, but they were already hard. 'You do remember what you promised me, don't you?' she said.

'How could I forget such a thing? Come.' He led the way out of the bedroom and along the corridor, the metal shutter closing automatically after them. In the atrium they mounted the wooden staircase and walked along the gallery to a broad hallway which ended in panelled double doors. He opened one and stood aside to let her enter first. 'Please...' he said as he gestured her through.

The room beyond was vast. There were two huge windows purporting to look out onto the lush tropical vegetation of the island, though in fact both were illusions much like those Corinda had seen earlier. Beneath them was a large dark blue sofa. The floor was tiled with marble and dotted with thick cream rugs, whilst the walls were lined with blue silk. At the back of the room was a double bed facing a small two-seated sofa, upholstered in a pale blue that matched the walls. The bed was lit by overhead spotlights. On a small table at the side of the sofa was a silver tray, a bottle of red wine and two glasses.

'Come over here,' he said. 'Would you like a glass of wine?'

'I think I would.'

He sat on the small sofa by the bed and patted the seat next to him.

'Constantine,' she said, kneeling beside him on the sofa, 'I've been thinking. You didn't kiss me last night. Can I kiss you now?'

He recoiled. 'I fear not. An unfortunate problem of mine, my dear. I should have explained. The skin on my face is especially sensitive. I can never indulge in the pleasure of kissing such beautiful creatures as yourself.'

'Oh, that's sad. I love kissing.'

He poured the wine and handed her a glass.

'Wouldn't we be more comfortable on the bed?' she said, aroused by his presence, memories of what they had done last night making her heart beat faster.

'Don't be impatient. I told you, I have a little treat for you first.' He clinked his glass against hers.

'What is it?'

'Something I think you'll enjoy.'

As Corinda wriggled round to sit on the sofa properly he clapped his hands. Almost immediately one of the two doors to the left of the bed opened and Iluska entered. She was wearing a short black satin slip and a pair of black stilettos, the heels of which were coated with chrome. She was otherwise completely naked. In her right hand she was holding a loop of leather attached to a metal chain, like a dog leash. The end of the leash was fastened to a ring, to which three thinner silver chains were attached. As Iluska walked forward Corinda saw these chains were secured to Irina's body and she was being led into the room by them. The upper one stretched to a silver choker around the brunette's neck, the other two to small silver clasps, like miniature hair-grips, the serrated jaws of which were firmly clipped to the girl's nipples. Irina was wearing only a pair of tight black leather panties and a pair of high heels identical to Iluska's.

Iluska led her to the bed, then dropped the leash. It fell and pulled on the nipple clips, making Irina gasp. Iluska glanced at Constantine, waiting for the signal that she should continue. He nodded and smiled.

'They take it in turns,' he whispered to Corinda. There were two wooden chests on either side of the bed. Iluska moved to the nearest and opened the bottom drawer. She pulled out a long strip of dark red silk. Turning back to Irina she wrapped it over the girl's eyes and tied it tightly at the back of her head. Then she unclipped the leash from the metal ring but left the other three chains attached to it. The ring came to rest under the girl's breasts.

Iluska barked a word of command in Albanian. The girl immediately crawled up onto the bed on all fours. The mattress was covered by a white linen sheet. Iluska patted her thigh to indicate that Irina should move round until her bottom was facing the sofa.

'She's beautiful,' Corinda said, almost to herself, admiring the brunette's toned buttocks partly covered by the black leather. Her nipples had reacted to the spectacle of the metal clips attached to Irina's flesh. She wondered what the clips would feel like, and the thought made her squirm her bottom against the sofa. 'What's she going to do?' she asked in a conspiratorial whisper.

'You'll see.'

Iluska knelt up on the bed alongside her companion, the satin slip floating around her body, barely covering her breasts. Very slowly she ran her right hand down over the small of Irina's back, over the black leather and down to her crotch. She stroked between her legs, moving her hand back and forth. Irina wriggled her buttocks almost imperceptibly.

As Corinda looked more closely she could detect indentations in the smoothness of the leather as Iluska's hand passed over it.

Another word of command was barked out. Irina immediately brought her knees together. Iluska reached to the waistband of the panties and began to draw them down over the girl's hips.

'Does this make you hard?' Corinda asked Constantine.

'Feel for yourself.'

She dropped a hand into his lap. His erection tented his trousers. She wrapped her hand around it and squeezed. It pulsed. The physical effect women exerted over men was interesting, she thought. It was power.

As the panties were peeled away she saw something was buried in the little puckered bud of Irina's anus. It was quite thick and had a flared base which fitted the contours of her body. As the panties were pulled lower a second object was revealed butting out of the girl's vagina, though the base was not flared and looked exactly like the dildo Arabella had given Corinda on her birthday. With the panties banded around Irina's thighs, Iluska seized both objects and pulled them out. Irina moaned. Two glistening dildos fell on the bed, both imitations of an erect cock, one shorter than the other.

Iluska picked up the larger of the two and sucked it into her mouth, licking the whole length of it. She appeared to find the taste of Irina's juices quite delicious. Irina, meantime, pulled the leather panties down over her knees and ankles and threw them aside. She then resumed her position on all fours, her knees spread apart again.

Corinda found herself staring at Irina's sex. It looked as if the scarlet-lipped orifice was breathing, opening and closing like a mouth gasping for air. She could see the thin silver chains too, hanging from her nipples and the choker, the metal ring attached to them, almost brushing the sheet.

Iluska rolled onto her back, abandoning the dildo. She insinuated her head between Irina's knees, then wormed her body around, under one of Irina's arms until her sex was immediately below Irina's head, with the satin slip rucked around her hips. She hooked one arm around the girl's back and levered her head up off the bed so she would get her mouth to the brunette's sex. Corinda could see her tongue licking greedily at Irina's clitoris. At the other end of the

58

equation Irina dipped her head between Iluska's thighs, and began to imitate the other girl's actions.

It was a kind of competition, each girl trying to give the other the greater pleasure. Iluska groped around on the bed and found the larger of the two dildos. She brought it up to Irina's buttocks and, without breaking the rhythm she had established with her tongue, found Irina's vagina and forced it inside.

Corinda saw the penetration make Irina shudder. It had exactly the same effect on her, provoking memories of how Constantine's cock had felt as it plunged into her for the first time. Most of what the girls were doing she had frequently done with Arabella. But she had never seen it before, never watched how the two bodies played against each other, the soft curves of breasts and buttocks melding together. The spectacle excited her intensely.

'Well, what do you think?' Constantine asked. 'Do you find this interesting?'

'It's exciting. It's made me so wet. Can I join in?'

He laughed. 'My dear, you may do whatever you wish,' he said, taking the glass of wine from her hand and putting it on the table. 'But first, to make it more interesting for you...' He delved into a pocket and brought out a strip of silk identical to the one Irina had tied around her eyes, except it was black. 'Turn your head.'

Corinda looked puzzled but obeyed. She could not understand why he wanted to do this to her but much to her surprise, as the black silk pressed over her eyes, closing out the light, she felt her sex surge with excitement. Her clitoris pulsed with renewed vigour, and the inner depths of her sex clenched as the precursor to a flood of juices. 'It makes me feel...' She tried to think of the right word.

'What, my dear?'

'Vulnerable.' It was the only word she could think of. It might even have been the right one.

'Stand up.'

As she stood in front of him she felt the satin robe being untied and slipped from her body. She moved slightly and felt his erection prod her navel. A hand brushed her nipples and she trembled. She felt him moving away and turned her head to follow the sound, but heard nothing further.

For what felt like a long time there was silence. There was no noise from the bed. Both girls had stopped whatever they were doing.

They were teasing her. 'Please, Constantine, do something. You promised, after all,' she said, frustration beginning to build in her body. 'I thought you wanted me.'

She heard a rustle from the bed and felt someone behind her. Two arms reached around and she felt two breasts crushing into her shoulders. As they were large, and covered in black satin, she knew they were Iluska's. Hands cupped her breasts firmly, then rolled her nipples between thumb and forefinger.

She had never been blindfolded before. She remembered how the darkness on her first night in this strange house had seemed to intensify her senses. It was the same now. Her nipples pulsed as Iluska's fingers pinched them. She arched her head back until it rested on the shoulder of the girl behind her.

'Make love to me,' she whispered, turning her head in the hope that the girl would kiss her. She got her wish. She felt an exquisitely soft mouth reaching awkwardly for her own, as the hands left her breast to stroke the strained sinews of her neck. Then Iluska turned her round by her shoulders, eager to get full contact with her mouth. As their lips met again Corinda's breasts squashed against the brunette's. She could feel Iluska's hard nipples, just as she could feel her own. She could feel the thatch of pubic hair too, such a contrast to her own, as the girl wriggled her pubis from side to side and her hand pressed tightly into Corinda's buttocks. Almost before she realised what had happened something hard and cold and slippery was being pressed between the cleft there, aimed not for the silky wetness of her vagina, but for the smaller orifice.

'What are you doing?' she said, breaking the kiss, her voice reflecting alarm and excitement too.

'There are so many things for you to learn, my dear,' Constantine said quietly, his voice coming from behind her. 'So many things I will teach you.'

The smaller of the two dildos nudged against her sphincter. She felt it resist, her buttocks rigid. With a conscious effort she tried to relax, wanting to learn a new lesson. Arabella had penetrated her there but never with anything but her fingers.

'Yes, that is good,' Constantine said, seeing her muscles relax.

The dildo slipped inside. Corinda felt a wave of sensation out of all proportion to the degree of penetration. A second, much stronger pulse followed as the dildo was pushed right into her, only the flared base preventing it from going deeper. The phallus in her anus generated pleasure that spread rapidly to her vagina and clitoris. They needed attention too.

And that was exactly what followed. She felt hands clasping her body, lowering her onto the bed, turning her on her back and pulling her legs apart. She felt hands and mouths everywhere; on her breasts, her thighs, her neck, her face. There was caressing and kissing, prodding and sucking; they made her writhe like a snake and toss her head from side to side, as she ground her buttocks into the sheet to keep the dildo deep inside her rear passage. She felt a tongue part her labia and light on her clitoris. She moaned loudly as, at exactly that moment, the head of the second, larger dildo nosed into her melting vagina and was thrust into it on the flood of juices her excitement had produced. Double penetration. She had never felt that before. Her mind immediately converted the plastic phalluses into animated cocks, since she knew what a cock felt like now. She had no idea if such a thing was possible, but it shocked her and sent her into a spiral of passion. All the new sensations her body was experiencing, accentuated by the blindfold and combined with the wicked fantasy her mind had conjured up, exploded in an orgasm; pleasure arched from the heads of the two intruders to her clitoris, where a tongue worked relentlessly, to her nipples, imprisoned in pinching fingers. Her body stretched across the bed, her hands and feet extended as if trying to reach for something, her muscles and tendons taut. Their rigour pulled her nerves taut too, so the music of her orgasm was played at a higher pitch.

'Now you, Constantine, please. I need it. You promised.' The first orgasm had again left her hungry for a second. She wanted desperately to feel what she had felt yesterday. 'Please.'

The hands left her body. She felt the larger of the two dildos being pulled from her vagina. A heavy weight moved onto the bed beside her. She opened her legs wider, if that were possible, and arched her buttocks off the bed, hoping Constantine would be able to see her urgent need. The weight moved and she felt her legs being lifted into the air. The unmistakable heat of a penis, Constantine's hard penis, butted into her labia.

'Yes, yes, yes. That's what I want,' she screamed, wriggling down on it until she managed to get it to the entrance of her vagina. A wave of desire overcame her, the anticipation almost as strong as the event.

'You need it, don't you my dear? You need it very badly, I think.' His voice was low and husky.

'You can see,' she gasped.

'Take it then.'

He slammed forward, falling on her, his fat cock skewering into her. The dildo had opened her but it didn't feel like this. Nothing did. Nothing ever had. This was the best feeling she'd ever had. She loved it. Adored it. Wanted more and more of it. But this was different from last night. The smaller of the two dildos was still buried in her anus and she could feel it alongside the sword of flesh thrusting into her vagina. Again she couldn't help wondering what it would feel like to have two cocks in there. Was that possible? She didn't know or care. The idea was enough. As Constantine began to pound into her, his buttocks moving up and down, the two brunettes held her legs up almost vertically to form a V. Corinda felt as though her sex was blossoming like the petals of a flower, opening to allow him into the very core of her.

'Yes, yes!' she screamed. Her whole body shuddered, wrapping around the steel-hard cock. She opened her mouth to cry out again but could make no sound. The feelings were too strong. In the blackness behind the blindfold she saw his cock driving in and out of her, parting her glistening wet flesh, ploughing into her alongside the plastic phallus in her rear, the two separated only by the thin membranes of her body. It was all in her imagination, but it was a vivid picture causing her to come again just as much as the physical stimulation. She was a woman now, a small voice kept repeating over and over, a woman in every sense. She felt her sex contracting around the hardness of his erection, gripping it tightly. Her clitoris pulsed wildly, and then a surge of raw pleasure rolled over her, making her gasp, wiping away everything but the feeling itself. Her hands clawed at Constantine's back, like a drowning girl clinging to a piece of flotsam.

The silk was unknotted and slipped from her eyes. She raised her head. The two brunettes were kneeling either side of her holding her legs. Constantine was poised above her, his arms straight, so he could look down her body as he pulled his cock almost all the way out of her sex. Corinda looked down too as it emerged, shining with her wetness, the gnarled veins of the shaft standing out prominently. She saw one of the girl's hands appear from behind his buttocks and fasten around the sac of his balls, holding it tight. Then as he dropped onto Corinda again, his weight crushing her, the view disappeared. She felt instead of saw his broad cock forcing its way into her again.

As he had done last night, this time he did not move. Instead he used all his energy to push, inching deeper. His cock began to pulse.

Only the second time, she thought. 'I want more,' she whispered in his ear.

She felt his cock jerk violently in the tight confines of her sex, as it spat semen into her. It was enough to set her off too, and she responded with such intensity that a third orgasm overwhelmed her. It was as strong as it was unexpected.

Corinda slept a dreamless sleep. She had the feeling, though she had no way of telling, that she woke early, her excitement breaking through her body's need to rest.

She lay in the darkness of the bedroom without switching on the bedside light, which now worked perfectly. She found herself thinking of Tim. Despite her gratitude to Constantine for everything he had done, and the mountainous sexual emotions he had aroused, she could not bring herself to feel the same way about him as she had about Tim. Tim had been so handsome and attractive. She couldn't help wondering whether it would have been different with him, whether her attraction to him would have added an extra dimension to her first experience of sex with a man.

She decided it would not. The pleasure had been so extreme she found it impossible to believe it could be improved upon. But it would have been different with him. She couldn't help wishing it had been Tim who had taken her precious virginity.

She began to think about last night, about the two girls and the dildos and the clips on Irina's nipples. She wondered if they were lying in each other's arms now, as the dawn broke, just as she had done with Arabella. She ran through everything that had happened, wanting to be sure she remembered it all. She felt her clitoris pulse. With no intention of doing anything but calming it she slid a hand over her naked belly, and slipped her middle finger into her labia. Her clit felt sore, but the soreness was not at all unpleasant. In fact it was provoking. She explored the little promontory. She felt a surge of pleasure from deep in her vagina, a sensation she had never had before, as if Constantine's penis had awoken nerves previously inactive.

It was a deliciously vicious circle. She should have turned on the light and gone to the bathroom to get ready for breakfast. She tried to tell herself, after the excesses of the last two days, that the last thing she needed was to masturbate. But the messages of pleasure her vagina was generating were too strong to ignore. They coursed into her clitoris which responded with equal vigour, and in seconds her nipples had stiffened to complete the circle, the feelings feeding off each other, her pleasure mounting. Then another element wanted to join in. Her mind. Her mind filled with images of male genitalia, of throbbing cocks and heavy balls, of smooth glans atop gnarled shafts. There were women too, with firm breasts and erect nipples. She imagined the puckered bud of an anus being forced open by a dildo, the lips of the brunette's labia spread around another phallus, and her own nether lips parting to admit a cock into the secret caverns that lay beyond.

'So good. It felt so good,' she said. 'So good.' She plunged her other hand down between her legs and thrust two then three fingers into her vagina, experiencing the same delicious soreness she felt in her clit.

'Fuck me, fuck me,' she sobbed, wanting to hear the words she knew would excite her.

She could almost feel Constantine plunging into her. She could feel the penetration in her anus too. She pushed a finger into her rear and wriggled it against the fingers in her sex. She thought she could still feel Constantine's semen inside her. She tossed her head from side to side with passion. Closing her eyes, the images in her head became more vivid. Faster than she could ever remember coming before on her own, all the strange new feelings her body was experiencing combined with the stark images that sprang up in her mind, created an orgasm. It was so sharp and sudden it was almost painful. She stretched out across the bed as though she were tied to some medieval rack, her muscles rigid, her head arched back, the sinews of her neck corded like rope. At that moment, as the orgasm played through the strings of her body, she saw Tim's face and his throbbing erection. She came for him.

The metal shutter had only been opened to bring her food. The woman in the black dress had brought her breakfast and lunch, exactly as she had yesterday, without saying a word. Corinda thought of following her out and going to find Constantine but, after what he had said she was afraid she might blunder into some part of the house she was not supposed to be in and accidentally open some door or window. The last thing she wanted to do was cause him pain. Not after all he had done for her.

So she remained where she was, reading, or trying on the outfits provided in the wardrobe. She paraded in front of the bathroom mirror in lingerie, trying on some of the more exotic garments the like of which she had never seen before. There was the whole range of make-up in the bathroom too, which she experimented with, trying darker eye-shadow, and blusher, and painting her lips with different shades of lipstick.

Even without the make-up she looked different. She stood in front of the mirror, looking deep into her own eyes and spotted, she thought, the mark of a woman buried within the mottled radius of her blue irises.

It was not, she guessed, until late afternoon that the metal shutter rolled up for the third time that day. This time her visitor was Eloisa. She was wearing a pair of tight denim shorts, so abbreviated that they cut across her buttocks diagonally, and a white cotton blouse knotted at her navel with all its buttons undone. As usual her outfit was completed by precipitously high heels, this time attached to white ankle-boots.

'I see you've found the clothes,' she said, as the metal shutter rolled closed. She looked around the room. Corinda had spread dresses over every surface.

'They are beautiful; I've never seen such things.'

'Constantine wanted to make sure you had the best.'

'He's so kind, isn't he?'

Eloisa smiled. 'He asked me to tell you, another guest has arrived.'

'A man?' Corinda asked enthusiastically, ever eager to expand her limited knowledge of the species.

'Yes, a Frenchman. He's going to join you for dinner tonight.'

'Oh, that'll be nice. I hoped I might see Constantine before then.'

'He's very busy at the moment.'

'I understand. It's just rather boring in here. Do you think I could go out for a walk?'

'I'll ask him. Constantine's very funny about that. He explained about his skin condition?'

Corinda nodded.

'I'll ask him though.'

'Can you tell him something for me? I've remembered the name of the solicitors. It was Morrison. Morrison and Morrison. Father and son. In London. Can he get in touch with them?' She had remembered the name suddenly whilst eating some figs she'd been brought as part of her lunch. In her mind's eye she could see the top of the stationery attached to the paper Tim had given her to sign, back on the island. Hopefully there would only be one such firm in London. Once they heard of her whereabouts they'd no doubt send a boat to get her. They'd have news of Tim too, and be able to tell Arabella she was safe.

'Morrison and Morrison?' Eloisa repeated.

'That's it.'

'I'll tell him.'

'He might be able to call them before dinner.'

'Do you want me to help you pick something to wear? Dinner will be in about an hour.'

'No, it's all right. I think I've worked that out for myself. On top and underneath,' she said, smiling coquettishly.

'Good. Have fun then.'

'Eloisa?'

'Yes?'

'Do you think Constantine likes me?'

'Sure. He likes you just fine.'

'Really?'

'Ah-ha.'

'You know, he let me have sex with him. And with Iluska and Irina.'

'Yes. He told me.'

'I hope I did it right.'

'I don't think you should worry about that. I really don't. I'll be back when you're ready to go.' Magically again the metal shutter rolled up and Eloisa left, the tight denim digging into the flesh of her buttocks as she walked.

Chapter Six

Constantine was standing by the roaring log fire. He had a small glass in his hand full of a cloudy white liquid.

'My dear, good evening. You must forgive me for not seeing you earlier.' Eloisa had told him of her conversation with Corinda, before she collected her and brought her to the main reception room. 'You look quite stunning,' he said as she walked across the room. 'I'm so glad we managed to find you something so delightful to wear.' He dismissed Eloisa with a nod of the head.

As Constantine took her hand Corinda felt her body throb. He touched his lips to her fingers; a touch as delicate as the brush of a butterfly's wing.

Corinda had decided on a daring black silk dress with a box neckline and a wrap-over skirt which split as she moved, to reveal a great deal of thigh. It even exposed the black lacy tops of the stockings she had carefully smoothed on her legs, and clipped into black suspenders. She thought Constantine would like the tantalising glimpses. She hoped it would remind him that she was more than willing to continue from where they had left off last night.

'You're drinking ouzo,' she said, recognising the aniseed smell of the drink Arabella loved.

'Would you like a glass?'

'I'd rather have champagne,' she said, spotting the wine cooler on the coffee table. She was developing quite a taste for it.

'Of course.'

He poured the wine and handed her a glass. 'Unfortunately I will not be able to join you for dinner tonight,' he said.

Corinda looked disappointed. 'Oh, Constantine, I thought we could...' It was not dinner she had in mind.

'I am disappointed, of course, but I do have a very charming dinner companion for you.'

'But I can't ask him to have sex with me,' Corinda blurted out, pouting.

'Oh, my dear. You underestimate yourself. With your qualities of persuasion I'm sure he will fall under your spell.'

'Really?' She brightened immediately. She had been fantasising all afternoon about what Constantine would do to her. But the prospect of having another man make love to her was, if anything, even more exciting.

'I think it's entirely possible.' He finished his drink.

'It's just that I've been thinking about you all day. I can still feel you right here.' She put her hand on her lower belly and pressed to show him the exact spot.

'We will renew our liaison, I promise you. But not tonight. I'm sure you will find Yves just as entertaining. He's anxious to meet you. And I've told him all about your miraculous escape.'

'Did Eloisa tell you I remembered the name of the solicitors?'

'Yes, indeed. Morrison and Morrison.'

'Did you get through?'

'I have asked my man in Athens to contact them as a matter of urgency.'

'I didn't mean to be ungrateful. It's just that I want to find out about Tim, and Arabella will be worried.'

'I understand perfectly. Ah, here is Yves.' Constantine turned to pour another glass of champagne as a tall man appeared at the atrium door. He was wearing black slacks and a black silk shirt, open at the neck. He walked across the room with an ease and grace that Corinda found fascinating.

'Yves Brice, may I present Corinda Chaste?' Constantine said.

'Enchanté, mademoiselle,' Yves said, taking her hand and kissing it much more firmly than Constantine had. 'It is a great pleasure to meet you.'

'And you,' Corinda said, feeling her heart leap. He was handsome. As handsome as Tim but in a different way. His face was rather long with bushy eyebrows and dark brown curly hair. He had brown eyes set deep under his brow, a straight nose and a fleshy mouth, his lips as smooth as a woman's.

'She is everything you said, Constantine,' he told the Greek.

'You are glad you made the trip?'

'Mais oui. A remarkable acquisition.' His English was perfect though his accent was unmistakably French.

'You make me sound like an oil painting,' Corinda said, thinking the way they were talking about her was strange.

'A very beautiful oil. A rare addition to anyone's collection,' Yves said, as Constantine handed him a glass of champagne.

'Only at the right price,' Constantine said. They looked at each other with a steady, meaningful gaze, but the meaning eluded Corinda. 'Forgive us, my dear,' Constantine went on, seeing her puzzlement. 'A private joke. Why don't you take Corinda into dinner,' he said to the Frenchman. 'As you know I must conclude some business.'

'That will be my pleasure.'

'Enjoy,' Constantine said before bustling away.

Yves took Corinda's arm and led her through to the dining room. As before the table was set for two, with all the necessary accoutrements sparkling in the subdued light. A large bowl of white Arum lilies had been set in the middle of the polished oak. The two Albanian girls stood by the serving door. They were a little more modestly dressed than at the last dinner, but still quite daring. Their gold lamé bodices were cut high on the hip, the crease of the pelvis visible at the front. The crotch of the outfits was narrow and did not cover the whole plane of their sexes. At the back it emerged as no more than a narrow thong, leaving their buttocks exposed. Their long legs were sheathed in shiny champagne-coloured tights and they wore gold high-heeled shoes.

As Yves helped Corinda into her chair at the table, Iluska fetched the champagne from the other room, and Irina disappeared through the serving door.

'Have you been here before?' Corinda asked as Iluska refilled their glasses.

'Yes, once or twice. Constantine usually thinks of me when he has something special.'

'What does he do exactly? I forgot to ask him.'

'I suppose you could call him a salvage expert. He salvages things then sells them on. To the highest bidder, naturally.'

'It must be very interesting.'

'Oh very.'

The dinner was French. There was a mousseline of sea bass and grenadine of veal, followed by a savarin, served with red fruits. The Turkish coffee was replaced by a lighter version flavoured with chicory. They chatted inconsequentially as the bizarrely dressed girls served the meal, though Yves's eyes, as far as Corinda could tell, never deviated once to look at them. He only had eyes for her. It was not until he suggested they take another glass of champagne that he mentioned the loss of her yacht.

'Connie tells me you were shipwrecked,' he said, as Irina poured the wine.

'Yes. He saved my life.'

'Is that so?'

'He's a wonderful man. He's been so kind to me. I'm afraid I've had a very sheltered life. Constantine has been teaching me all about sex.'

'About sex?'

'Yes. I suppose I shouldn't have asked him really. After all he's done.'

'You may leave us now,' Yves said, looking at the two girls standing by. They nodded and left. 'You asked him what, exactly?'

'To have sex with me. I'd never done it before. And he agreed. Wasn't that nice of him?'

'Yes, it most certainly was.'

'It's so different from being with a woman.'

'Being with?'

'Having sex with.'

'You've had sex with women?'

'Yes.'

'And which do you prefer?'

'I like both. They're very different. Is it the same for a man? I mean, is it very different having sex with a man, than with a woman?'

'I've never had sex with a man,' Yves said.

'Why not?' Corinda looked surprised. The sexual mores of men needed a lot of explanation. This was an area her biology lessons had not covered.

'It is not so easy for a man. Other men do not excite me like women do.'

'You mean you don't become erect? Tumescent?'

'Precisely.'

'But you've tried?'

'No. Never. There would be no point. What excites me is the softness and femininity of women; their breasts, their legs, the curves of their buttocks. Men are hard and ugly.'

'You're not ugly.'

'Not to you.'

'I'm glad I can do both,' Corinda said, sipping the champagne. It was cold and refreshing.

'What do you like most about women?'

Corinda thought for a moment. 'I love it when they lick my clitoris. I love that.' She squirmed slightly at the thought.

Yves smiled. Everything Constantine had told him about the girl was true. She was totally innocent and totally uninhibited. 'What about if a man licks your clitoris?'

'That hasn't happened yet. Do you think it would be different?'

'It might be.'

Corinda looked at him steadily. She loved those big brown eyes. 'Do you think I'm beautiful, Yves?'

'Mais oui.'

'Have you got an erection?'

He almost choked on his coffee. 'Would you like it if I had?' he asked, regaining his composure.

'It would mean you're attracted to me, right?'

'Yes.'

'That you want to have sex with me? Do you want to have sex with me?'

'I'm very attracted to you.'

It was Corinda's turn to smile. The thought of having sex with Yves was appealing. He was older than Tim but in many ways just as attractive. But she was coming to realise that she was a beautiful young woman and that beauty bestowed on her a certain power when it came to men. At least that was her theory, and Yves represented a chance to put that theory to the test.

'Perhaps I don't want to have sex with you,' she said, though it was exactly the opposite of how she felt.

'That would be a pity.'

'The thing is...'

'Yes?' he said eagerly.

'The thing is, there's certain things I'd like to do.'

'Like what?'

Last night Corinda had been subjected to an assault on her senses, the hands and mouths of two women and a man whipping her into a frenzy of passion. But it had only been a taste. Her imagination had run riot with possibilities. From an educational point of view it had only been the tip of what she suspected was a very large iceberg. She knew precisely what she wanted next and it was not something she felt she could ask of Constantine. She had asked so much of him already. But Yves presented her with a means of extending her sexual awareness.

'Perhaps I should go back to my room,' she said coquettishly, deliberately teasing him, wanting to see how strong her power over him was.

'Don't do that. I'll do anything you want,' Yves said. It was true. The girl was incredibly exciting. She had a unique mixture of innocence and sensuality.

Corinda got to her feet. The skirt parted to reveal the tops of her thighs, the taut suspenders stretched over the creamy flesh above the black stockings. She saw his eyes staring and deliberately moved her legs so the view disappeared.

'What I'd really like...' She licked her lower lip.

'Yes?'

'What I'd really like is to see a man with another woman. Making love with a woman.' Last night she'd seen two women together for the first time. It was exciting because she could visualise, from angles she'd never seen before, what she and Arabella had looked like together. She wanted to have the same privilege with a man, so she could see what it looked like as a penis forced its way into a woman's sex. It was partly curiosity, but mostly the desire to be able to picture it in her mind's eye when it happened to her again.

'Would you do that for me?'

'Of course, what man would not?' Yves could think of nothing nicer.

'With any woman I want?'

'Naturally.'

'You know Eloisa?' Corinda had found it difficult to forget what had happened with the American in her bathroom. She could still feel the woman's delicate touch. She hoped, after she'd watched her with Yves, she could be persuaded to renew the passion they had shared. Of course she wanted the Frenchman too, but she could see no apparent reason why she could not have both.

But Yves's enthusiasm evaporated. He had been imagining one of the Albanians. Eloisa was not the sort of woman he found attractive. She was too well-built; too powerful. 'But she's not interested in men,' he protested.

'Isn't she? Do you mind if I take my dress off? I'm not really used to wearing so many clothes.'

'Of course not.'

She unzipped the dress and pulled it off her shoulders. She had found a red and black satin basque amongst the lingerie. It fitted her narrow waist tightly and laced up the front. She had discovered that the tighter she laced it the more sexy it made her feel, though she had no idea why. Its bra was a little on the small side, making her breasts swell, pushing them together to form a deep cleavage. She had not bothered with panties.

'You were saying?' she said, pleased at the way his eyes were devouring her.

'She's not into men,' he said, his voice hoarse.

'Let's go and ask her, shall we?' she suggested. 'If she won't agree then we'll have to think of something else to do. I'm sure we can think of something, aren't you?'

Yves couldn't tear his eyes from her. 'You're very beautiful,' he almost whispered.

'Mmm...' Corinda was enjoying her part, seeing the effect she was having on the Frenchman. 'I feel hot.' She ran her hand up her thigh to her pubes, then thrust her middle finger between her labia. 'I get wet so quickly. Do you think that's normal?'

'Come here, let me see,' he said.

She took two steps towards him as he pulled his chair out from under the table. He put his hand on the lacy stocking top and moved it up between her thighs.

'Naughty,' she said, slapping it away. 'You said see, not touch.' Yves caught her hand, pulled her onto his lap and kissed her, squirming his lips against hers and plunging his tongue into her mouth. She felt a surge of passion. She got up and pulled him to his feet. 'Let's go and find Eloisa.'

'How do we do that?'

She picked up the bell used to summon the servants. She rang it and Iluska appeared, taking no notice of Corinda's state of undress.

'We need to find Eloisa,' Corinda told her. 'Can you take us to her?'

Iluska nodded. 'Please to follow,' she said. She turned and walked out into the sitting room, and through to the atrium. Leading the way up the wooden staircase she took them along the gallery, passed the corridor that led to Constantine's bedroom, and into a narrower longer passageway. At the far end she stopped and pointed to a door, before turning and walking back the way they had come, her high heels clicking on the tiled floor.

He knocked on the door with his fist. They waited. There was no reply.

Corinda tried the door handle. It was not locked. She opened it. 'Eloisa,' she said, leading the way inside.

The light in the corridor had been bright in comparison to the light in the bedroom, which was dimmed. As they closed the door behind them it took two or three seconds to adjust their eyes to the surroundings. The room was not large. There was a bookcase on one wall, crammed with books, and a small desk and chair against another wall. On the opposite side was a large wide bed.

Eloisa was kneeling on it, on all fours. Kneeling behind her was a short-haired blonde girl, her hands gripping Eloisa's hips. She was naked, her body slender and tanned with pert breasts and pert buttocks. Her face was pretty, with round grey-blue eyes and a petit nose. She was naked but for a leather harness that banded the tops of her thighs and her waist. Secured into the harness at her groin was a life-sized plastic phallus. It was poking between Eloisa's labia, which had pursed around it.

Yves walked to the side of the bed to get a better look.

'Did I tell you to stop?' Eloisa snapped. The blonde had frozen the moment the two entered the room.

'What are you doing?' Corinda asked, fascinated, as the blonde bucked her hips and the phallus slid into Eloisa's sex, then pulled out again.

'Just having a little fun. Since you're here, pick up that whip and warm her up a bit for me, would you honey? She's flagging.'

'I'll do that,' Yves said quickly. There was a riding crop lying on the edge of the bed. Now Corinda's eyes had fully adjusted to the light she could see there were several red stripes across the blonde's buttocks. Yves raised the whip and swept it down across the blonde's bottom. The impact caused her to stab the phallus into Eloisa's sex.

'Mmm...' Eloisa wriggled down onto the dildo.

'Is that exciting?' Corinda asked, wide-eyed. She wasn't sure whether she meant Eloisa to answer or the blonde.

'Come here,' Eloisa said. 'Come here and kiss me.' She doubted if Constantine knew Corinda was here. He had expressly forbidden her to initiate any more sexual contact with the girl, but this was different. Perhaps it was Yves' idea. He was here to audition the girl, after all. Not that she cared. She was quite happy to take advantage of the situation. Constantine could hardly complain if she helped him clinch the sale.

Corinda sat on the side of the bed, then crawled forward until she could kiss Eloisa on the lips. Her tongue explored the woman's mouth. It was hot and wet.

'Can you feel it?' Eloise asked huskily. 'Can you feel how aroused that thing makes me?'

'Yes.' The sight of the two naked women so strangely coupled was affecting Corinda strongly. She could feel the familiar stiffening of her nipples and the churning of her sex. The tightness of the basque seemed to exaggerate the feelings, making them more acute.

With a flick of his wrist Yves landed another stroke across the blonde's buttocks. The girl bucked forward, pushing the phallus home. Eloisa's mouth was pushed forward by the impact. It butted against Corinda's lips and they kissed again hungrily.

Whatever Corinda had expected it was not this. Her heart was pounding. Asking Eloisa to have sex with Yves while she watched would have to wait. She had other more pressing priorities now. Quickly she rolled onto her back. She wriggled under Eloisa until her belly was directly below the American's face, her head wedged between the blonde's thighs. In this position she stared up into both women's crotches, their sexes joined by the plastic dildo.

Immediately Eloisa dipped her head to Corinda's sex, and found her clitoris with her tongue as unerringly as a compass finds true north. She heard Corinda moan.

As the initial shock of pleasure ebbed away Corinda felt her clitoris being agitated. Her whole body began to tingle. She watched as the blonde bucked her hips and the phallus sunk more deeply between Eloisa's labia, stretched so tautly around it. The blonde had very little pubic hair and Corinda could see her sex lips clearly. There was a thin leather strap extending down from the lower angle of the plate, which disappeared into the girl's sex. Wanting to give as well as to receive, a principle Arabella had instilled into her, Corinda manoeuvred her arms around the girl's thighs and levered her face up until she could get her tongue between her labia. She had to push the leather strap aside to get at her vagina.

Thwack! Yves lashed out with the whip again. The three females were so closely joined it affected them all simultaneously; the jolt of pleasure tinged with pain arced through them like an electric shock. It created a circuit. The sudden thrust of the blonde's hips forced the phallus deep into Eloisa's vagina. That caused her to exclaim with surprise and delight, expelling hot breath against Corinda's sex. Corinda in turn was jolted by this surge of pleasure against the blonde's vagina, her tongue burrowing deeply. This encouraged the girl further and so the circle was complete. Another lash followed, as intense as the last, and produced the same result. The three reacted in unison, their bodies synchronised in the ring of passion, the excitement mounting.

Corinda had never experienced anything like this. Eloisa's tongue moved her clitoris with an inexorable rhythm which would have made her come on its own. But there was so much more. There was the feeling of the blonde's wet vagina and the taste of her juices, and the sight of her quivering labia. The shock of the whip had established a means of communication between the three of them and now other sensations were following the newly opened path. What Corinda did to the blonde, by licking and thrusting her tongue as deep as she could into the girl's vagina, was communicated to Eloisa through the unyielding cock. Eloisa's mouth, in turn, pressed to Corinda's sex, sent the message back to where it had come. They created a spiral of passion that was winding itself tighter and tighter. The rhythms were the same. The heat was the same. And after no more than a few seconds, so were their orgasms.

Corinda knew she came first. It was too much for her to bear. Everything that had happened to her over the last few days, the voyage of sexual discovery she had willingly embarked on, from the moment Arabella had thrust the dildo into her melting vagina for the first time, to the moment she had taken Constantine in her mouth and her sex, and all the exciting events in between, seemed to combine. As Eloisa's artful tongue swept across her clit her body arched up off the bed, her eyes forced closed, and a surge of raw sensation coursed through her in waves, reaching a crescendo that seemed to last forever.

Somewhere, in the midst of orgasm, she felt Eloisa come too, shuddering at exactly the same moment the blonde's body went rigid and her sex contracted around Corinda's tongue. But she was only aware of it for a second as the demands of her own orgasm became too consuming to allow her to concentrate on anything else.

How long it was before the sensations died away she could not tell. She opened her eyes and saw the blonde pulling the dildo from Eloisa's sex. It made a plop as the shaft disengaged, and Eloisa's labia folded back on themselves. Eloisa rolled onto her side.

'Well, you do learn fast,' she said. There was a bottle of wine on the bedside table. She got to her feet and poured herself a glass. She drank it in one gulp, her hand trembling slightly. 'So to what do I owe this honour?'

'My idea,' Corinda said, sitting up.

'And?' Eloisa looked at Yves. A bulge distended his black slacks. Though he was not short and she, for once, wore no heels, she was still taller than him.

'Yves wanted to have sex with me,' Corinda said.

'Well, you are very beautiful.'

'So I set him a little challenge.'

'A challenge?'

'I wanted to watch him with you first. I've never seen a man with a woman. I thought it would be good for my education.' She wanted to see it even more now she had seen Eloisa penetrated by the artificial cock. 'Would it turn you on?'

'I think it would.' Eloisa reached down to Yves's crotch and took hold of his erection. 'I don't usually do straight sex with men,' she said. 'But if you ask real nice, I suppose I could make an exception. Since Corinda's been so good to me. Say please.'

'Please,' he said. Any reservations he may have had, had quite disappeared after what he'd just seen.

'Good boy. Get your clothes off.'

Yves began unbuttoning his shirt. Eloisa snapped her fingers and the blonde, divested of the dildo now, sprang to help. She undid his belt and unzipped his flies, then pulled his trousers and boxer shorts down to his ankles, freeing his rampant cock.

'What's that?' Corinda exclaimed, pointing at the ring of skin that still partly covered the Frenchman's glans, as he pulled off his shoes and socks.

Eloisa laughed. 'A foreskin.'

'What's a foreskin?' Corinda asked. She vaguely remembered the term from her biology lessons, but neither of the men she'd seen so far had one.

'Some men have it cut off at birth,' Eloisa explained. She reached down to Yves' cock and pulled his foreskin back, making him moan. 'See.'

It was extraordinary, Corinda thought. Suddenly Yves' penis looked like the other two she had seen; the glans pink and swollen, with a distinct ridge separating it from the shaft.

Eloisa poured more wine, drank half a glass, then lay back on the bed. Facing the Frenchman she slowly opened her legs, her muscular thighs parting to reveal her sex.

'Do you think you'll be able to manage me?' she asked. She spread her legs further apart until her labia opened. In comparison to her dusky complexion the inner surfaces of her sex were a light pink. She bent her knees and arched her buttocks off the bed, angling her sex towards him, while her hands kneaded her breasts. 'Are you going to fuck me? I don't give many men the chance.'

Yves dropped to his knees on the bed. He took her right leg in his hand and began caressing it, then bent forward to kiss the inside of her thigh. He worked his way down to her open sex and tongued her clitoris.

'Get on with it,' she said irritably, pulling his head away by his hair. 'You're here to fuck, not suck.'

The Frenchman straightened up then rolled on top of her, his cock sinking into her wet vagina at the first attempt.

'Is this what you wanted to see?' Eloisa asked Corinda. 'Or this?'

The American wrapped her arms around his back and scissored her legs together tightly, forcing them underneath his and trapping his penis inside her, then rolled over until he was on his back and she was on top of him. She then brought her knees up so she was straddling his hips. The whole manoeuvre was accomplished with his cock still embedded inside her. Raising herself on her haunches she let Corinda see his erection, now slick with her juices, slide almost all the way out. She then dropped, impaling herself, and ground her clitoris against it.

Corinda watched with fascination as the American rose again, and Yves' cock reappeared. She moved round to get a closer look, her sex throbbing as she watched the penis ploughing into Eloisa's vagina. It looked exactly as she had imagined it would; exactly like the image she'd formed in her head while Constantine had been plunging into her. That is why she'd wanted to see it, so that next time she would be able to see in her mind's eye, as well as feel, what was being done to her.

As she leant forward her leg brushed against the discarded dildo. It was still wet. She picked it up. 'Use it on her,' Eloisa snapped at the blonde, her movements becoming more urgent. She bounced up and down on Yves with considerable power. Her fingernails raked across his chest. 'Not bad for a man,' she said.

The blonde took the dildo from Corinda's hand then pushed her over until she was kneeling on all fours, as Eloisa had been earlier. She did not strap the dildo on again. Instead she held it in her right hand and guided it between Corinda's labia as her other hand stroked the curve of her buttocks.

The sight of the penis being enveloped in Eloisa's sex had given Corinda a new sense of arousal. She wanted the dildo very much. As soon as she felt its tip at the entrance to her vagina she wriggled back on it, and the wetness her sex had produced allowed it to slip into the depths of her body. She pushed back strongly, wanting the phallus as deep as it would go, then used her internal muscles to grip it, just as she had gripped Constantine's cock the previous night.

The dildo didn't have the heat and pulsing life of the real thing, but it still produced waves of glorious feelings. The blonde began to pull it down, but Corinda reached back and grabbed her wrist, pushing it up again. She didn't want a stroking rhythm. She wanted total penetration. She wriggled down on it, and felt its hardness right in the core of her, as her eyes closed with the jolt of pleasure.

Eloisa's voice broke through Corinda's reverie, and she forced her eyes open to watch. She saw the Frenchman's cock slamming up into the woman as he bucked his hips off the bed, matching Eloisa's movements. From the expression on her face the American was close to coming. Suddenly she forced her weight down onto him, not allowing him to buck up off the bed again, and as Corinda watched, ground her hips from side to side as her fingers clawed at her own nipples. She was looking straight at Corinda, displaying herself with eyes sparkling, showing her what she wanted to see.

'Jesus,' she screamed, her eyes screwed closed as her body went rigid and her orgasm took hold of her.

It was too much for Corinda. The feelings the artificial phallus created were doubled by the empathy she felt for Eloisa. Her sex contracted, her muscles stretched and her orgasm exploded, making her cry out too. The image of the Frenchman's penis ploughing between Eloisa's sex lips stayed in her mind, long after her eyes had been closed by the flood of exquisite sensation.

She waited for her orgasm to drain away, but before she could open her eyes she felt hands grabbing her by the hips. The dildo was pulled from her, leaving her tingling, and then the unmistakable heat and hardness of a cock replaced it, thrusting into her with a startling urgency. Its slickness and the juices of her own body combined to make the penetration frictionless. It reared up into her, deeper than the dildo had. She felt hands groping her breasts, fingers tugging them clear of the basque and kneading the flesh, while others found her nipples and played on them too. As the cock drove in and out of her another hand ran up her stockinged leg and caressed the creamy thigh above as it worked up to her clitoris. It was swollen and tenderised by everything that had happened. A finger, whose she did not know, stroked it with no real gentleness or finesse.

Despite the mountainous waves of pleasure she forced her eyes open. Eloisa was lying at her side. The blonde was kneeling next to her, driving the phallus, that a few seconds earlier had been inside Corinda, into Eloisa's sex from the back, while she played with Corinda's breasts with her other hand. As she watched Eloisa wriggled forward slightly, got her mouth close to Corinda's breasts and opened wide. The blonde fed Corinda's nipple into it. Immediately Corinda felt a new wave of pleasure, as the American sucked and licked and nipped the tender flesh between her lips. Her other breast was being kneaded by Yves.

Another orgasm was exploding through her, wiping out her ability to do anything but wallow in bliss. Somewhere, buried in the middle of all the provocations her mind and body were prone to, there was one crystal clear image that seemed to be at the centre of everything; a picture in her mind's eye of Yves's cock, forcing its way between her labia and deep into her sex, a picture not based on what she could see but on what she had seen as she'd watched him with Eloisa. Now she knew exactly what it looked like - another lesson in her sexual education was complete.

Suddenly the speed of his thrusting increased. The fingers that dug into her hips became like steel. She felt his muscles harden. As she came out of the depths of her own orgasm she felt his beginning. Unlike Constantine he did not stop plunging into her. She felt his cock jerking in her vagina and tried to squeeze it with her sex, but it did not stop and his semen erupted as he plunged in and out. Long after the last spasm had jetted spunk into her he was still moving, though more slowly. Finally he stopped and withdrew, his cock nudging against her buttocks and leaving a wet mark there.

It took some time to recover. She had come three times, each time more forcefully than the last, and she was deliciously exhausted. She would be sore again tomorrow, of that she was sure, but she looked forward to it; it would be a wonderful reminder of what had happened, of what she had learnt, and of what she had become.

She lay on the bed and rolled into a ball, not wanting to get up. It was as though she were surrounded by a fog of euphoria, and she wanted to stay enveloped in it for as long as possible.

She was vaguely aware of the blonde leaving and Eloisa pouring a drink. They had gone over by the desk, and were talking in whispers. Corinda did not have the energy to listen to what they were saying, but odd phrases lodged in her mind.

'...Might get to like it, baby...' Eloisa said.

'It was not my idea.'

'Not bad.'

'...Better than I imagined,' Yves said.

'Next time perhaps... prefer a more intimate arrangement.'

'She's not as...'

Corinda thought she might have dozed off to sleep, but when she came round they were still talking. She was too comfortable to move and remained curled up.

'So what shall I tell Constantine?' Eloisa asked.

'Tell him I'm interested.'

'How interested?'

'You want me to name a price?'

'Of course.'

'Thirty thousand.'

Eloise laughed. 'Are you joking?'

'It's a fair price.'

What they were talking about now Corinda didn't know. It was obviously business of some sort and that didn't interest her. She was more interested in whether Eloisa would let her spend the night here. Despite having no windows the room was less forbidding than her own quarters, and it would be comforting to share a bed with the American, as she had done so many times with Arabella.

'There are other bidders.'

'What other bidders?'

'Two, at least.'

'Thirty-five, then. No more.'

'And the blonde?' Eloisa asked.

'I didn't come here for her.'

'But since you've seen her? You can see how well I've trained her.'

'I'm not interested. I like to do the training myself. That's what makes this one so fascinating.'

'Exactly. But you won't get her for thirty-five.'

Corinda found all this very puzzling. They seemed to be talking about her. But perhaps she'd dozed off and missed something. Yachts were called 'her' too, and she was sure they were probably talking about some vessel Constantine had salvaged.

'Forty then,' Yves said after a pause.

'Is that your final offer?'

'Yes.'

'I'll tell Constantine. Pity.'

'Why?'

'Because it won't be enough. And I'd have liked to see her go to you.'

'I've never known you be sentimental before.'

'There's something special about this one. Sure you won't change your mind?'

Yves shook his head. He went to the bedroom door and let himself out.

Chapter Seven

'My dear, may I introduce an old friend from Athens? This is Dimitri Boutos.'

'I'm charmed to meet you, my child. Charmed indeed.' Dimitri Boutos was small and stout. He was middle-aged, with a full head of black hair which looked as though it had been dyed. Like Constantine he wore only an open sports shirt and a pair of white cotton slacks.

Constantine had sent word for Corinda to join them for lunch. She had dressed in a simple white silk shift and white high heels, in order to give herself more practice at walking in them, and because they had become associated in her mind with her newly emerging womanhood. They were uncomfortable but that was a small price to pay. She felt adult in them. She felt confident in them. They reminded her of how far she had come in the last three days.

They were in the garden. It was not a garden in the true sense, as it was not open to the sun. But a huge conservatory had been constructed to one side of the house, where with the aid of specially designed propagation lamps that gave the illusion of sunlight, and reflective glass, tropical and semi-tropical plants grew in a riotous profusion of colour. French windows led from the main house on to a stone-flagged terrace and it was here that Corinda was greeted by Dimitri and Constantine.

'You have not seen my garden,' Constantine said. A large butterfly, with jade-green and magpie-blue wings, fluttered by and alighted on the foliage of a large acacia growing in a terracotta pot by the terrace doors. 'We breed the butterflies in a special hothouse. There are thirty-six varieties.'

'It's wonderful,' Corinda said as she watched the green and blue wings take to the air again, and fly up to the glass panels where they settled on a metal stanchion supporting the roof.

There was a white cast-iron table and white chairs with bright green cushions. A bottle of ouzo, a glass jug of water, an ice bucket, and several small glasses were set on the table.

'A glass of ouzo before lunch perhaps?' Constantine said.

'Thank you.'

The woman in the black dress who had collected Corinda from her room poured the drink for her and refilled the men's glasses, dropping in more ice.

'What do you say in English? Bottoms up?' Dimitri raised his glass. His eyes had not left Corinda for a single second.

'Is Yves going to join us?' Corinda asked.

'No, my dear. Unfortunately he is a very busy man. He has been called away on business. Unavoidable, I fear. He asked me to offer you his apologies. I have been telling Dimitri all about your extraordinary upbringing.'

'Yes. Most fascinating,' Dimitri said.

Corinda realised he was only the fourth man she had ever met face to face. But, unlike the others, his presence had not produced a sexual pulse in her. She found that curious, destroying her theory of chemical reactions between men and women. Perhaps it was the result of the orgy of sexual emotions she had experienced last night with Yves and Eloisa. The fact that she had not been allowed to spend the night in Eloisa's bed had given her more time to dwell on what she'd felt. She had spent the morning in a sort of daze, the soreness she had anticipated in her sex and nipples a constant reminder of the ecstatic pleasure she had reached. Her disappointment at not seeing Yves again was probably a factor too. She had found him a very attractive man. She could not say that of Dimitri.

'I'm afraid,' she said, trying to be positive, not wanting to let Constantine down, 'it means I haven't had much experience of men.'

'So I understand.'

'Though Constantine has been so kind to me.'

The two Albanians arrived. They carried trays of food: salads, bread, cheeses and fruit. Wine was set on the table and Corinda was helped into her chair by Dimitri. After breakfast and last night's dinner Corinda, for once, was not hungry and ate sparingly, though Constantine and Dimitri devoured the food.

'Is there any news?' she asked as she toyed with forkfuls of chicken mayonnaise.

'My agent has not called yet. If there is no news after lunch I will call him again.'

'Thank you. I am worried.'

'You were shipwrecked?' Dimitri said.

'Yes.'

'And what have you been doing with your time on the island?'

Corinda laughed. 'Completing my education.'

'In what respect, my child?'

'My sexual education. Constantine has ensured I have been given some very valuable lessons. I suspect he even asked one of this friends to help me out.' She was sure Constantine had primed Yves, asking him if he'd mind taking her to bed in his place, so as not to disappoint her. 'Is it true?' she asked him.

'I might have mentioned something of the sort.'

'You see,' she said to Dimitri, her point proved.

'I certainly do.' Dimitri's eyes had fixed on the way Corinda's breasts pushed against the material of her dress. The top two buttons were undone and he could see the curves of soft flesh, nestling in a lacy white bra. 'I have always found Constantine a prince among men.'

'Perhaps Dimitri here might be willing to help too,' Constantine suggested. 'He is free this afternoon. We have a little business to conclude but that won't take long.'

'The boat is coming for me at five,' Dimitri said.

He took another swig of red wine, wiped his mouth on a napkin and stood up. 'But until then...'

'So there is no time to lose. My dear...'

Corinda looked from one man to the other. It was clear she was expected to go with Dimitri. Constantine obviously thought the idea would appeal to her, but despite her desire to please him and her gratitude, it did not. For the first time in the brief history of her relationship with men, she felt no thrill of anticipation at the thought of sex. Not that she felt she could refuse, however. After saving her life and everything else he had done, a refusal would be churlish.

'I have something special in mind,' Dimitri said, offering Corinda his hand to help her to her feet.

'It will be a new experience for you,' Constantine added.

'I've had a lot of those recently,' she said, trying to appear more at ease than she actually felt. 'Will I see you later, Constantine?'

'Of course.'

He watched them go, waving as they got to the terrace doors. Dimitri lead her up the staircase and along the corridor to a door not far from Constantine's bedroom.

'You are very beautiful, my child,' he said as he opened the door and they walked inside. The bedroom was comparatively small and had no windows. It had a double bed, a single bedside chest, and an antique mahogany wardrobe. The floor was made from strips of polished oak, with a single white rug by the bed.

The mattress of the bed was covered with a black sheet. Lying at the foot of it was a snake's nest of straps and leather harnesses.

'May I undress you?' Dimitri asked.

'Yes.' If Constantine had said that to her, or Yves or Eloisa, the words would have produced a distinct thrill of sexual excitement. As it was she felt nothing.

She watched as the Greek's stubby fingers undid the buttons of her dress. As it parted his eyes feasted on her breasts, confined in the white lace bra. Dimitri's hands trembled slightly as he unbuckled the cotton belt at her waist and unfastened the two remaining buttons. She was not wearing panties.

'Beautiful,' he said, staring at her belly and the short blonde hair of her pubes. 'Quite lovely.'

'I'm glad you think so,' Corinda said. She could see a bulge forming under the fly of his trousers. She was getting used to the effect her body had on men. It was a sort of power. She pulled the dress from her shoulders and let it fall to the floor, then reached around behind her to unclip her bra. Leaning forward she let the bra straps fall to her arms, but held the cups against her breasts with both hands.

'Do you want to see them?'

'Yes,' he said.

She dropped the bra, her breasts quivering. 'Well?' She cupped them in her hands.

'They're lovely.'

For the first time she felt a tinge of excitement. What she was doing was turning her on, even if he wasn't. She had always assumed in the complex sexual nexus between a man and a woman, that it was the man who was in control. She had learnt that a woman had just as great an ability to create desire and passion and need, and what's more, could get pleasure from doing it. She turned her back on him and bent over, thrusting her buttocks out. She spread her legs apart, giving him a good view of her sex. Keeping her left hand around one breast, she ran her right down between her legs, and used a finger to spread her labia apart.

'And do you like this?'

'That most of all.'

'So what is this special experience?' she asked, straightening up and sitting on the edge of the bed.

For a second he did not reply, momentarily dazzled. Constantine was right. She was very special, her innocence making her uniquely salacious.

'Kneel on the bed,' he said.

'Are you going to fuck me? I know all about that.' She climbed onto the bed and knelt on all fours. She felt her clitoris throb. 'Like this?' she asked, wriggling her bottom at him and spreading her knees further apart.

'No.' He took her by the shoulder and pulled her up so her back was straight. Then he picked up one of the leather harnesses. He wrapped a leather belt around her waist and buckled it tightly. Another strap, slightly thinner, wrapped underneath her breasts and a third above them, both buckled at the back. All three were connected by thin straps running down her sides.

'What's this for?' she asked, puzzled.

'Put your hands behind your back,' he said, ignoring her question. His voice had changed. It was remote and unemotional, betraying no tenderness or any other feeling.

The tightness of the straps he had already applied made her slightly breathless. Attached to the back of each of them were two leather cuffs. The top two were further apart than the two below them, which were further apart than the two below them, which were touching each other. As Corinda held her arms behind her back he buckled the cuffs around her upper arms, then just above her elbows and finally her wrists, making it impossible for her to move her arms in any direction.

'What are you doing to me?' she asked.

'It is what pleases me.'

Just as she was going to ask why she found a leather pad being thrust between her lips, gagging her. The pad was cigar-shaped and attached to a metal ring at either end. These were connected to a leather strap that he secured behind her head.

'Stand up,' he ordered.

With difficulty, not having the use of her arms for balance, Corinda crawled to the edge of the bed and climbed off it.

Dimitri studied her bound body. The straps above and below her breasts had constricted them and they had turned a light pink. He touched the right nipple lightly with the tip of a finger and saw Corinda shiver, the constriction increasing its sensitivity.

He picked up a leather collar from the bed. Attached to the front of it was a chain leash. He buckled the collar around her neck at the back, the chain leash swinging down across her breasts. It was cold. She couldn't believe her nipples could get any harder, but the touch of the metal made then stiffen again.

'Does it excite you, child?' Dimitri asked, aware of the frisson the chain had caused.

She nodded. She had no idea why but the tightness of the straps excited her very much, just as the tightness of the basque had.

'Then I have taught you something today. You have learnt your first lesson in bondage. An ancient art. For years men and women have taken pleasure in binding their slaves, in depriving them of their ability to resist whatever fate might befall them. He started to undress, kicking off his shoes and stripping off his socks. He unbuttoned his shirt. 'No one knows why many have been so attracted to the practice, but it has been documented even in the earliest civilisations.' He pulled off his shirt and undid his trousers. A large erection distended his black briefs. 'Of course it blossomed in the nineteenth century, so we are led to believe. The French and the English had bordellos with rooms devoted to increasingly complex ways of rendering a lady or gentleman completely helpless. It seems to have been a passion. Some would say a perversion, common to both sexes. It is, no doubt, a response to a profound psychological need buried in the psyche. But where and what, we shall probably never know. I have devoted many years to finding an explanation, but none of the great clinicians or psychologists I have studied have managed to explain the deep-seated significance bondage seems to play in the human sexual condition. It is, perhaps, enough merely to accept that it does and be content to enjoy its very real delights.'

He skimmed his pants down his short legs and stepped out of them. His erection was large, out of all proportion to his rather stout body, and very smooth, the shaft almost as featureless as the glans. It was a young man's cock, more like Tim's than the others she'd seen. Corinda felt a sharp pang of lust.

'At home,' he continued, 'I have a special room and have designed my own equipment; some of it, I dare to say, original. Perhaps you will have an opportunity to test it for yourself. But at the moment, as we are here, I will have to content myself with introducing you to more primitive means.'

He was looking straight into her eyes. He used the knuckles of his right hand to stroke her strap-divided cheek.

'Bend over, my child. It's time for your next lesson.'

Dimitri's hand pressed down on the back of her neck until her head was level with the tops of her thighs and the chain leash dangled vertically from the collar. Using her hips, he guided her round until the leash was brushing one corner of the bed.

'Perfect,' he said. He dropped to his haunches and wrapped the leash around the bedpost several times, knotting it loosely but effectively enough to prevent her from straightening up.

He got to his feet again. She heard him opening the wardrobe door. He walked back to her. She could see his feet just behind her legs.

'You did not lie, did you?' Something cold ran over her buttocks and down to her labia, parting them. She knew what he was referring to. She knew her sex was wet. The position she found herself in excited her.

'The other element that has puzzled the collective mind of so many distinguished psychologists and observers of the human condition, is why so many people should be sexually excited by the idea and the fact of pain. It is, you will find, yet another leitmotif that runs through civilisation, like a golden thread woven into the complex material of life.'

His hand gently caressed her buttocks. The touch made her flesh tingle. Whatever he had used to part her labia was sawing up and down between them.

'The sexual enjoyment of pain, is a double-sided coin of course. It is often as enjoyable to give as to receive. Of course we are talking of a specific type of pain: pain that is administered solely for the purpose of pleasure.'

If she had not been gagged she would have begged him to fuck her. The movement between her sex lips was making her clitoris pulse and the sexual energy this generated seemed to be magnified by her bondage. Her breasts throbbed, tightly sandwiched between the two straps. She desperately wanted to feel that smooth cock slide into her sex. Couldn't he see how wet and open she was? What was he waiting for?

The room was silent. His hand left her buttocks and whatever had been between her legs was withdrawn. She heard him take a deep breath. Suddenly there was a swish of air, a loud *thwack*, and a stripe of heat seared across her naked bottom. Almost before she had time to work out what it was a second *thwack* followed, and in the time it took to raise his arm again, a third. The gag muffled her scream, the leash preventing her from rearing up.

'You see,' he said quietly.

To her astonishment the pain from the three weals turned almost instantly to something else; a type of pain certainly, but one that sent messages to her sex of an intensity and power that was almost indistinguishable from pleasure. She remembered how the blonde's body had felt as Yves wielded the whip last night, how it had responded with squirming sensuality to every stroke. She found herself moaning and wriggling her bottom from side to side.

The second shock was even more extreme. Dimitri laid his hands on the red weals he had made, stroking them lightly. That was exquisite. Corinda had felt no pleasure like it. The hands felt cool, like balm, but at the same time they provoked renewed pangs of that peculiar pain-striated pleasure. She shuddered. She felt his finger running down between her buttocks to her labia.

She mumbled incoherently, fighting the gag. Suddenly her body spasmed, and the heat from her buttocks become more intense. His finger slid against her clitoris, a jolt of pleasure combined with the sensations the red marks were generating and an orgasm broke over her, taking her completely by surprise. It was not like the orgasms she had experienced before. It seemed to be inextricably involved with the heat in her bottom, and provoked sharp pulses of sensation wherever the whip had landed. It was as though each of the weals had become as sensitive and as capable of sexual response as her clit.

'You see?' Dimitri repeated, watching her body tremble.

He drew his hand away, then pressed his cock into the cleft of her buttocks. She could feel its heat. It was throbbing. It was exactly what she had felt with Constantine and Yves; the prelude, she knew now, to ejaculation, except they had been buried inside her, while Dimitri was only rubbing against her bottom. She wriggled against her bonds, trying to push his penis down between her legs, but he held her by the hips to prevent it. Not that her movement didn't excite him further. She felt his cock jerking more violently, and then a trail of liquid splattered over her lower back. A second wave, with less energy, landed on her red-striped buttocks.

Dimitri did not move for a long time. Corinda felt the semen dribbling down her buttocks and the backs of her thighs.

83

'Please,' she tried to say through the gag, shaking her head to remind him she was there. The bondage was no longer exhilarating, and a cramp was developing in her shoulders.

Eventually she felt his hands working at the buckles of the harness. He freed her arms then unbuckled the collar around her neck so the leash fell to the floor and she could straighten her back.

Despite her orgasm, for the first time in her sexual relations with men, she felt used. None of what Dimitri had done to her was intended for her pleasure. He had bound and whipped her not to excite her, but because it was what he wanted. He had caressed her buttocks and her sex not for her satisfaction, but only to increase his. He had been careless of her needs, and the excitement she had experienced was purely incidental.

He threw the whip on the bed. It was braided leather with a loop at its tip. She picked it up.

'What were you saying about it being as enjoyable to give as to receive?' she asked. 'I think that should be my next lesson, don't you? Only seems fair.' Her eyes were sparkling but it was with anger not excitement.

Dimitri had pulled on his briefs and was stepping into his trousers. 'Perhaps another time, my child. I have a boat to catch.'

'There's plenty of time for that.' Corinda stood with her legs apart, the three leather straps still secured tightly around her body. She was determined not to let anyone treat her as Dimitri had done. She had so little experience of men she had no idea whether what had happened was common or not, but she knew enough about herself to know that no man would ever do that to her again. It was not the bondage or even the whipping, both of which had excited her in a way she would never have imagined, but the way he had ignored her needs and concentrated only on his own.

Dimitri tried to pull his trousers up over his thighs but as he did so she pushed him in the back and he toppled onto the bed. Before he realised what was happening she pulled his feet up onto the mattress and was sitting on his shoulder. He was not used to physical exertion. Corinda, on the other hand, was young and fit, her body honed by running along the island beaches and swimming out to sea. It was not difficult for her to resist his struggles and keep him pinned to the bed.

'Now let's see if you're right about the enjoyment.' She lashed the strap down across the meat of his fleshy buttocks. They quivered and a red weal appeared instantly. He tried to wriggle out from underneath her, but she held him firmly and delivered a second harder stroke, allowing her anger to feed through to her arm. The third blow was even more intense.

Dimitri moaned. He stopped struggling. She raised her arm again. The whip slashed down and she heard that unique sound of leather against flesh; the *thwack* she had heard for the first time last night. Dimitri moaned again but his tone had changed.

'Again,' he hissed, his face buried in the black sheet. 'Again. Do it again...'

84

Corinda did not hesitate. She swept the leather down a fifth time, and then a sixth for good measure, crisscrossing his buttocks with bright red stripes and little scarlet bruises where the tip bit into his soft white flesh. Then she threw the whip on the floor and pulled herself off him.

Dimitri rolled over. He was grinning, his cock erect again. On the black sheet where he had been lying was a gooey white puddle.

'It seems the experiment was a success,' he said.

Corinda could not sleep. At first she'd fallen asleep with ease, exhausted by the conflicting emotions of the day. But she woke again after no more than an hour, and lay in bed in the dark unable to doze off again. Her mind was racing, trying to digest everything that had happened, her many worries crowding in on her.

She was worried about Tim most of all. Constantine obviously knew the waters around his island, and she was desperate to believe him when he reassured her Tim would be all right. But she had begun to have her doubts. The thought that Tim was dead, that she would never see him again, made her break out in a cold sweat. Of the men she had met in the last few days none compared to Tim. Constantine had been kind to her, and Yves was handsome in his way, but neither had given her the same sort of emotional charge she had felt for Tim. From the books she had read, and from the classics of English literature, she gained the impression that sexual satisfaction went hand in hand with sexual attraction. But with the experience she had gained over the last few days she had begun to realise that sex and sexual attraction were two different things. She could have one without the other. She had not been attracted to Constantine at all, but had found the things he did to her sexually overwhelming. Yves was more attractive and certainly gave her a wonderful feeling of sexual fulfilment, but he was not a man she would have chosen for herself. Tim, on the other hand, was very much to her taste, and she regretted that they had not been able to consummate their sexual encounter. She was not sentimental but she did regret he had not been the man to take her virginity.

Thoughts about him led to thoughts about Arabella. She knew she would be worried sick and she missed her terribly. She was so grateful to her for introducing her to the joys of sex, though she realised it was probably in contravention of her father's wishes. She had felt innocent and gauche in Constantine's hands, but would have been that much more so if she'd not gained some experience with Arabella.

But it was getting off the island that preoccupied her thoughts the most. She had not seen Constantine again yesterday, so she did not know whether his agent in Athens had any more news. But she couldn't help dwelling on the conversation she had overhead between Yves and Eloisa. She couldn't get it out of her head, however absurd the idea, that the price Yves had mentioned was something to do with her. And then there was the remark Dimitri had made. It stuck in her mind too. When he'd been talking about whether she'd have the opportunity to test his specially equipped bondage room, he'd said that was what he had come for. What on earth did that mean? She had thought he'd come to the island on business.

Why, also, was she kept locked in her room? Yesterday, after she'd left Dimitri, was the first time she'd been unaccompanied in the house. She found her way back to her room and discovered the switch that operated the metal shutter. But some automatic mechanism closed it the moment she stepped inside. She wished now she had taken the opportunity to explore the strange windowless house. She was sure it held secrets she could not even guess at. That was the only reason for her virtual imprisonment. Surely Constantine could not really believe she would let light in, even accidentally?

All these thoughts rolled around in her head, coming and going, one worry replaced by the next, until eventually she drifted back into an uneasy sleep.

It seemed only minutes later that the shutters woke her and Eloisa strode into her room. She was dressed in skin-tight cream leather trousers and an equally tight matching leather halter that left her back bare. As usual she wore high heels, though this time they were white leather boots.

'Constantine wants you to have breakfast with him,' she said.

That was a new development. Up until now breakfast had always been served in her room. 'Do I have time for a shower?'

'I'll come back in five minutes.'

'No, stay. There are some things I'd like to ask you.' Corinda got up from the bed and went into the bathroom. She used the toilet, cleaned her teeth, then climbed into the shower. This was a good opportunity to ask some direct questions.

'Is something bothering you?' Eloisa asked, standing in the bathroom doorway.

'I don't know what's happening. What were you and Yves talking about the other day?' Corinda asked, wrapping herself in a towel as she stepped out of the shower.

'I thought you were asleep.'

'No, I heard.'

'It was just business. Constantine's business.'

'What sort of business?' Corinda rubbed her legs dry.

'Yves buys and sells like Constantine. He is bidding for a piece of merchandise Constantine has acquired,' Eloisa said quickly.

'What merchandise?'

'A sculpture,' she lied. 'An Egyptian head. It's not really legal, I guess. It should never have been taken out of Egypt. It's very valuable.'

'And Dimitri?' Corinda rubbed her breasts dry and discarded the towel. She applied some eye-liner.

'What about Dimitri?'

'He seemed to think I might be going to visit him.'

'Visit him? What do you mean?'

'He said that was what he'd come to arrange.'

'You must have misunderstood. Dimitri is here for the same piece as Yves. They're rival collectors. Perhaps he was just hoping you'd agree to go and see him some time when you're back in London. He has an apartment there. He's very impressed with you.'

Corinda looked into Eloisa's eyes to see if she could find the truth there. But she could not. She turned to the mirror and applied a little eye-shadow, a touch of blusher and a coat of red lipstick, then walked passed Eloisa into the bedroom. 'What shall I wear?'

'Something light.'

She took a pretty blue shift from the rail in the wardrobe and dropped it over her head. She shook out her long blonde hair then brushed it. There were some dark blue high heels which complemented the outfit. 'Ready.'

'Right. Let's go.'

The shutter started to roll up. Previously Corinda had taken no notice but now she wondered how Eloisa had operated it when there was no switch to be seen anywhere in the room.

Constantine was sitting at the table on the terrace in the conservatory, giving the impression he was basking in the bright sun. He got to his feet as soon as the two women approached.

'Good morning, my dear. How charming you look. So young. So fresh. Please be seated. There are some fresh figs which I recommend.' He indicated the table which was laden with fruit, a jug of orange juice, coffee, milk, a bowl of yogurt, and two baskets of sweet breads and croissants. 'Please help yourself.'

Corinda was hungry. She sat at the table and reached for the figs.

'You may leave us,' Constantine said to Eloisa.

'Of course,' she said, trying to indicate with her eyes that Corinda had asked some awkward questions. Constantine shook his head as if to dismiss the problem, so she left them.

'So, my dear, you slept well?'

'Not really.' Corinda bit into a croissant and poured herself a glass of orange juice. 'I wanted to ask you about London. Have you contacted the solicitors?'

'I am pleased to say that problem is solved.'

'Solved?'

Constantine smiled. His gold teeth caught the artificial light. 'Yes. My agent in Athens has had a great deal of trouble getting a telephone number for Morrison and Morrison. But meantime I have managed to contact an old friend of mine. He has been cruising in the Mediterranean and happens to be passing by. He is on his way to London. I explained your predicament and he will be delighted to help. His yacht will berth here this afternoon. Tomorrow you can depart with him. He'll take you to London. I'm sure from there it will be easy to find the executors of your father's will.'

'Really?' Corinda said excitedly, her fears evaporating to be replaced by a wave of relief.

'Absolutely. He is only too pleased to help, I can assure you.'

'Oh, that's wonderful. I really have been so worried.'

'Of course you have. That is natural.'

'I can't thank you enough, Constantine.' She had been stupid, she told herself; stupid ever to doubt him. In the watches of the night worries got exaggerated, she knew. She had simply misunderstood some casual remarks.

'It's entirely my pleasure, my dear. I have work today, I fear, but tonight I shall send for you again and hopefully by then the prince will have arrived.

'The prince?'

'Yes. My friend is a prince. A small nation in north Africa. His father is their king. One day Samora will inherit the throne.'

'A real prince?'

'And a very rich one. His country may be small but it sits on large deposits of oil and platinum. Samora's family is extremely wealthy.'

'I can't wait to meet him.'

'Has anything else been bothering you, my dear?' Constantine sipped his coffee.

'No, no. It was just that...' Now he had found a way for her to get to London it seemed ungrateful even to mention it.

'Please, you must tell me if anything is distressing you. I realise the conditions here are far from perfect for someone so young and vigorous, but you will understand my condition means...'

'No. It's not that Constantine.' She touched his arm. 'It was only Dimitri. It was really kind of you to let your friends have sex with me. I appreciate it, I really do. But Dimitri was...' She shuddered at the thought of him.

'Dimitri hurt you?'

'No, not really hurt. I suppose I don't know what to expect from men, that's all. He didn't treat me like you have.'

'You will never see him again, I assure you.'

'Good.'

Dimitri had offered more than Yves. Constantine had almost concluded a deal with him until he had received a call from the prince via his satellite phone. In fact the prince was the first person Constantine had tried to contact about his latest acquisition but his yacht had only just put into port and he hadn't got the message over the radio. He had asked Constantine to wait for his arrival. If the girl was everything Constantine said she was, he would double Dimitri's offer. Constantine was so sure Corinda would appeal to the prince's taste he told Dimitri the deal was off.

It would be a pity to see her go, of course, but business was business after all.

'So finish your breakfast. Enjoy the sun. There are sunbeds on the first floor, if you would like to make sure your tan is topped up,' he said. He wanted her to look her best for the prince.

'Really? Can I do that?'

'Of course.' He got to his feet, took a final sip of coffee, and wiped his lips with a white linen napkin. 'You'll have to forgive me.' He turned to walk away, then stopped. 'Oh,' he said as an afterthought, 'wear something seductive. I'm sure you'll want to make a good impression on the prince.'

'Don't worry, I will.'

Chapter Eight

Corinda spun around in front of the long mirror on the bathroom door. She was much more adept in the high-heeled shoes now and could walk quite normally without tottering. She had topped up her tan on the sunbeds, as Constantine suggested. Then she used the afternoon deciding what she was going to wear, and experimenting with her make-up. She applied mascara to her long eyelashes, and eye-shadow which made her look, she thought, less youthful and more sophisticated. A touch of blusher on her cheeks emphasised her cheekbones, and a deep red lipstick defined her perfectly symmetrical mouth.

Her hair had been pinned up, to leave her lithe neck bare. She hoped that, since this was to be her last night on the island, Constantine would agree to go to bed with her. She had selected her lingerie as carefully as her dress. Among the many beautiful things she'd found in the wardrobe was a garment she thought matched his description of what was seductive. It was made from an almost transparent black material, tight and stretchy. It hugged her breasts and the hem dipped into four triangles, from which hung black suspenders. The garment had no hooks or zips or laces. It had to be smoothed, pulled and inched into place.

In contrast to its confining hug her buttocks and sex felt open and free. She decided to wear panties, reasoning that it would be alluring, at the right moment, to let Constantine watch her wriggling out of them. There was a pair in the same semi-transparent black. They were tiny, only just covering her pubis at the front, and with nothing at the back but a thin thong.

Knowing Constantine's predilection for them, she wore stockings. She chose a pair of sheer black with a welt which the suspenders pulled into chevrons on her thighs.

Her dress had been more difficult to choose. After she'd squeezed into her underwear she tried on several possibilities among the glittering silk, satin and lace creations that - though she did not know it - had been looted from the wrecks of many yachts. In the end she chose a strapless blue affair that shimmered with tiny sequins and clung to her as tightly as the corset. It displayed her ample cleavage and her curvaceous figure to the best advantage, and its modest ankle length gave no hint of the secrets she wore underneath. With black suede high heels and a dab of a musky scent Eloisa had provided, her outfit was complete.

The picture in the mirror was very different from the girl who had arrived on the island four days before. She examined herself from every angle. She like the way the fitted waist of the dress flared out on her hips and clung to her pert bottom and the upper contours of her thighs.

Her days on the island had not been wasted. With the wardrobe of clothes and make-up at her disposable she had taken the chance to learn what suited her and what didn't, what flattered and emphasised the positive, and what made her look less than her best. Up to now clothes and her appearance had been a matter of no concern to her. But on Constantine's island, among the many lessons she had learnt, she realised exactly how important appearance was, especially in relation to men. She learnt that what she wore under her clothes was just as important as what she wore on top. She had discovered that make-up could be used to set a mood too. It was all part, she was sure, of being a woman and not a girl. As she stood gazing at herself in the shimmering dress she was very much a woman now, in every sense.

And she was ready.

She walked back into the bedroom and sat on the bed. As well as there being no natural light in the building there was very little sound either. The insulation that prevented light leaking in clearly prevented sound too. Though she had tried she hadn't heard the slightest noise from outside; no wind or sea, and certainly nothing to indicate whether the prince's yacht had arrived and he'd come ashore.

She tried to read but the words refused to register. Her mind was too full of questions. What would the prince look like? Would he find her as attractive as the other men did? It would be a long voyage to England and she hoped he might want to take her to bed. She was eager to continue her lessons at the school of sexual manners.

It seemed to be hours before she jumped to her feet as the shutter motors ground into life. The woman in the black dress beckoned her out and led the way through the house, not to the main reception room as Corinda had expected, but up the staircase and along the hall to Constantine's bedroom. The woman knocked on the door twice and retreated back down the hall without waiting for it to be opened.

Corinda stood waiting. She thought she heard voices inside. The woman had disappeared by the time Constantine came to the door.

'My dear, you look enchanting,' he said. He was wearing a green velvet robe tied at the waist with a plaited silk cord. He stepped aside and gestured her in. 'Would you like a glass of champagne?'

'Thank you, that would be nice.' She had expected him to be dressed for dinner, but tried not to register surprise that he was not.

There was a wine cooler on the coffee table. He indicated that she should sit. He poured the wine and handed her a glass, then refilled his own.

'Salute,' he said, raising his glass. He sat in a button-backed wing chair upholstered in the same dark blue as the sofa on which she sat.

'Has he arrived?' she asked anxiously, fearing that not being taken to the dining room meant a change of plan.

'Oh yes, he got in this afternoon. He'll be here in a moment. He's very anxious to meet you. I thought a more intimate setting might be appropriate. We can dine later, if you don't mind.'

As they were alone she decided to broach a matter that had been bothering her. 'I hope you didn't think I was ungrateful, complaining about Dimitri.'

Constantine smiled, then put a finger to his lips. 'Not another word. The matter is forgotten.'

There was a knock at the bedroom door. She felt her heart leap.

Constantine smiled at her again. 'Well, your prince has come.'

He got to his feet and went to the door. She had her back to it and didn't want to appear too anxious to twist around and look, so she sat demurely with her hands in her lap, having deposited the glass on the mirrored coffee table in front of her.

'Come in, my friend, come in,' she heard Constantine say. Footsteps walked across the marble floor. 'Corinda Chaste, may I present Prince Samora Laraki?'

She stood up and turned to face the newcomer. She felt her heart skip a beat. He was handsome. Very handsome. He was tall and slender, with the grace and natural poise of an athlete. His skin was black, not mahogany or even chocolate, but ebony black. His face was symmetrical, balanced around a delicately straight nose and high, sharp cheekbones. His lips were thin and smooth, and his chin firm and chiselled. His eyes were hypnotic, perfectly proportioned and elliptically narrow. They were the colour of burnt amber, their whites flawless and in stark contrast to the colour of his skin. His hair was black too, the tight curls cropped to his scalp.

'It's a pleasure to meet you,' he said, in an accent that reflected its English public school origin. He extended a slim hand. His fingers were quite thick and his nails manicured. He wore a large gold signet ring, with a crest engraved on it.

'And you,' Corinda said, a little overcome. She wondered if she should curtsey. She felt a thrill of sexual excitement as he shook her hand.

'Constantine said you were an exceptional beauty and, of course, he was quite right. If you don't mind me saying, you are exquisite.' For a second his eyes left her to look at the Greek, letting him know he was very pleased.

'That's very kind of you.' Corinda had been gifted with so many compliments on the island she was starting to believe them.

'Some champagne?' Constantine said, sitting down again and pouring the prince a glass.

As seemed to be the fashion among Constantine's guests, Samora was wearing slacks and a shirt. The slacks were navy blue and the silk shirt was the palest of pinks. He took the glass and sat on the sofa next to Corinda. She could smell a strong, musky cologne.

'Constantine told me of what happened to you,' the prince said.

'Would it be possible for you to take me to London?' she asked.

He looked momentarily nonplussed. Then he smiled broadly, revealing a set of perfectly white, perfectly regular teeth. 'Oh, London, of course. That's no problem.'

'I'd be so grateful. Constantine saved my life, you know. Has he told you that?'

'He's told me all about you,' Samora replied, looking at her intently. 'So we are to travel to London together.'

'That would really be very kind. Look, I don't have much experience with men, so I hope this doesn't sound strange, but you really are very attractive. I don't suppose you'd consider having sex with me on our voyage. It is a long way.' She would have liked to have sex with him now but she wasn't sure whether Constantine was intending to make love to her, since he was only partially dressed and they were sitting in his bedroom.

The prince laughed lightly. 'She's delightful, Connie, just as you said.'

'You're making fun of me.'

'No, no, my dear,' the prince said. He put a hand on her knee. The touch was like an electric shock. 'It is simply that you are so charming. I would be happy to have sex with you. If you want the truth, I feel so attracted to you I'd be happy to begin right now.'

'An excellent idea,' Constantine said. 'Why don't you two get to know each other properly?'

'You don't mind?' Corinda asked.

'Certainly not.'

It was so typical of him, she thought. He always seemed to have her best interests at heart. He could probably see how attracted she was to the prince.

'But one thing first,' the prince said. 'I have a little surprise for you.' He got up with almost balletic grace, went to the door and opened it. The two girls had been waiting outside. 'For you, Connie,' he said as he beckoned them in. 'A little present to keep you happy this evening.'

The girls were both black, both naked apart from a silver choker around each of their necks and silver bracelets around one wrist. A chain was attached to a ring at the front of each of the chokers and looped between the girls. Another shorter chain linked the left bracelet of one girl to the right bracelet of the other. In their untethered hands each held what at first appearance looked like a stubby wooden sword. It was only as they got closer that Corinda saw that the blade part, protruding from the handle and wooden guard, was a carved replica of an erect penis.

'They are lovely, Samora, lovely.' Constantine got to his feet to inspect his present.

It was true. Both girls were slim and voluptuous. They had long legs and their hips snakelike, their buttocks pert. Both had short black hair. Both had pubes which had been trimmed neatly. Their breasts though were different. One had small breasts with stiff little nipples, while the other had large round breasts with large round nipples.

The prince clapped his hands. 'Enjoy,' he said, sitting next to Corinda again.

As if following some rehearsed plan, the larger-breasted girl dropped to her knees in front of Constantine. She parted his velvet robe and buried his cock in her mouth, as the other girl walked behind him, trailing the chain from the chokers around his shoulders. She unknotted the sash of the robe and pulled it off, leaving him naked. Then she pressed her body into his back, running her fingers over his barrel chest to his nipples. As she sucked and kissed his neck her fingernails pinched the tender flesh and Constantine moaned.

The spectacle made Corinda's sex moisten. She didn't know whether it was responding to the naked girls or to the sight of Constantine's erection bobbing in and out of the kneeling girl's mouth.

'Are you shocked?' the prince asked, sipping his champagne.

'No,' she replied. What a strange question. The suddenness had surprised her, and perhaps that was what he was reading in her expression, but to be shocked she would need to have standards of behaviour by which to judge. As the only standards she had formed, when it came to relations between men and women, had been based on what she had seen on Constantine's island, the behaviour of the two girls seemed perfectly normal. 'They're very beautiful,' she said seriously.

'Yes, they are.'

'Watching makes me feel...'

'What?'

'Excited, here.' She pressed her hand in between the tops of her thighs.

'Does it feel nice?'

'It would feel a lot better if you kissed me,' she said.

'You excite me,' he said. He brushed his tongue against her lips, then sank his mouth on to hers. His tongue plunged into it. She squirmed her lips against his greedily.

'Does that make you erect?' she asked as he pulled away.

He smiled. 'Of course.'

'Does it?' She pushed her hand into his lap and felt a hard ridge unfurling in his trousers. 'I'm new at all this,' she explained. 'You have to teach me what you like.' She unzipped the fly and delved inside. Parting his shorts she found his erection. It was hot. She didn't think she'd ever get used to how hot men's cocks felt to the touch. She pulled it out of the trousers and gazed at it unabashed. It was large and, though the shaft was the same black as the rest of his body, the glans was bright pink.

'No foreskin,' she said, almost to herself.

'I lost it at birth,' he said.

'It's big.' She grasped it in her fist and squeezed. The glans inflated. She relaxed her grip then squeezed again. She leant over and slipped it between her lips, sucking the tip before opening her mouth and plunging down on it. She heard the prince moan.

'No, no,' he said, pulling her off him.

'Did I do something wrong?'

'No, of course not. I just like to take it more slowly. I'd like to look at you first.'

She understood that. She had spent most of the afternoon preparing, though she had imagined it would be Constantine she'd undress for. Getting to her feet she glanced across the room. Constantine was lying on his side on the bed, with one of the girls in front of him and one behind. Corinda resisted the temptation to watch, wanting to concentrate on the prince. She reached behind her and pulled down the zip of the dress, turning so she could look into Samora's eyes. 'Is this what you want?'

She began to wriggle the dress down her body. As it descended her breasts were revealed, the black material of the corset veiling her flesh but not hiding it. She pushed the dress down her hips until it fell around her feet. She stepped out of it, picked it up and draped it over one arm of the sofa.

His eyes roamed over the glories of her body; the swell of her breasts, the narrow waist, the creaminess of her thighs above the taut black stocking tops, and her panties, the softness of her pubic hair visible inside them. She was a beautiful girl. He had purchased women from Constantine before, but none of them had been like this. She was a prize. Money, he determined, would be no object.

'Is this what you want?' she repeated. She sat on the mirrored surface of the coffee table. In the short history of her sexual experience she didn't think her sense of anticipation had been so keen. She wanted to feel that hard penis penetrating the depths of her sex. She wanted to feel it pounding into her and ejaculating. She knew the desire was mutual. She could see it in his eyes.

Bringing her knees up she pushed herself back on the table until her shoes were resting on its surface. She parted her knees. She ran both her hands down over the black nylon until they were resting against her sex. The crotch of the tiny panties had folded into the crease of her labia. Through the black material the prince could see her pussy lips.

Slowly she pulled the panties aside. With the middle finger of her right hand she peeled her labia apart and found her clitoris. The first touch made her gasp. She looked up at the prince. 'Is this what you want to see?' she said as she pushed three fingers into her vagina.

'Lovely,' he said, his eyes riveted to her sex and the mirror image of it immediately underneath. He watched the fingers slide in up to the knuckle, then out again, slick with her juices.

'Am I doing the right thing? Does this excite you?' She didn't really need to ask. She could see his cock pulsing.

'Very much,' he said quietly without looking at her face.

'I'm making myself come. Do you want to see that?' It was true. The obvious effect she was having on him, the power she was wielding, was definitely an aphrodisiac.

'Yes,' he breathed, transfixed.

She looked down again. She could see her fingers pushing into her vagina.

She stroked her clitoris with her thumb and felt her body churn with excitement.

The prince got to his feet. He tore his clothes off, throwing them aside. His body was hairless and muscled. The pubic hair around his cock was thick and wiry.

'Wouldn't you rather have the real thing?' he asked.

'Let me come for you like this,' she said, increasing the rhythm of her fingers, an orgasm close.

The prince dropped to his knees in front of her. He took hold of her ankles and lifted them over his shoulders. Then he leant forward so his mouth was almost on top of her sex. 'Let me do it then,' he hissed.

Corinda pulled her hands away. Samora's tongue darted out, forcing its way between her labia. It found her clitoris easily. It was hard and swollen. No man had ever done this to her. She almost orgasmed at the thought. Firmly his tongue circled the little nub of flesh as three fingers moved to her vagina. They penetrated slightly, then spread apart, stretching her open. The tight circumference of her sex responded, pulsing, rushing her closer to the brink of an orgasm.

The wetness from her sex ran down between her buttocks. She felt another finger pressing against the ring of her sphincter. That produced a thrill of pleasure, but as her sphincter relaxed and he pushed inside it instantly doubled. She remembered how the dildo had felt, but this was totally different. His finger was wriggling inside her energetically, pushing as far as it would go and moving from side to side. Then she felt him plunge into her vagina too. She wasn't sure how many fingers were buried in her. She only knew they were lined up side by side, plunging in and out in unison.

'Make me come...' she managed to gasp.

She felt herself falling back until she was lying on the table, her head tilted back over the edge. Her body was falling too, an orgasm sweeping over her, the sensation pulling her down into a pit of mind-numbing pleasure, as his fingers burrowed into her and his tongue stroked the nub of her clitoris.

Suddenly the fingers were pulled from her sex and she felt herself being picked up. The force of her climax had closed her eyes. She opened them to see the prince hooking his arms around her back and lifting her off the table as, with seemingly no effort, he got to his feet. His hands slipped under her buttocks and, with her legs wrapped around his back, he positioned her sex over his vertical erection. Gradually he lowered her onto it, his cock burying itself in her vagina.

'Oh God,' she murmured. She threw her arms around his neck and kissed him full on the mouth, her tongue dancing against his.

She slipped further down his body, until she could feel the base of his cock against her clitoris. Then he bucked his hips, propelling his cock even deeper. His hands held her buttocks, his fingers like cups of steel. Though she knew he was supporting her weight it seemed as if she was hooked on his cock.

He felt wonderful. His cock filled her. She found she could lever herself up on him and then drop back. She thought she would come again. She would certainly come again if he ejaculated. She squeezed him with her vagina.

'I want you,' he said.

'Take me then,' she told him.

Gently, without pulling out of her, he sat on the edge of the sofa and unwound her legs from around his back. Then turning to the side he leant back and put his feet up. It left Corinda straddling his hips.

She wriggled over him slightly so she could get both knees on the sofa cushions, then raised herself until his cock was almost disconnected from her. She held it there. Then she sank down on him. She remembered Tim. This is exactly what she had been so close to doing with him.

She remembered something else too. Reaching behind her back she groped for the sac of his balls, just as one of the Albanians had done with Constantine. As she slid up and down on his cock she pulled his scrotum. She concentrated, trying to use everything she had learnt to please him. She used her vagina to squeeze the length of his shaft, then ground her clitoris against its base, the hardness of it making her body shudder anew.

He looked up at her. The gauzy black material still held her breasts in a tight grip, but the soft upper slopes of them trembled as she moved. He reached up and pulled the cups down, then pressed his fingers into the pliant flesh and erect nipples. He was going to come. She would be his. He would own her. Possess her. She would be his to command.

Corinda established a rhythm. She found she could use her vagina to milk him when he was deep inside her. Milk him. The idea excited her. Milk him of his spunk. She rose up on her haunches, then slid down again, then squeezed him with the muscles of her sex. The squeezing provoked huge pulses of pleasure, each enough to send her back into another orgasm. But she resisted. She had more control now. She knew what to do to hold herself back. She knew how to give him pleasure. She could feel his cock jerking inside her.

He abandoned her breasts for her thighs, running his hands over the stocking-tops until he felt the smoothness of the flesh above them. He couldn't fight the urge to come any longer. He bucked up off the sofa at exactly the moment she sank down onto him. In the maelstrom of ecstasy he knew his coming had made her come too, the feelings feeding off each other, taking them both higher and deeper into their own sensibility.

Corinda's second orgasm was more powerful than her first but, as so many times on Constantine's island, it left her wanting more. As she felt the prince's cock soften and slide out of her she got to her feet. She picked the bottle of champagne from the cooler and poured herself a glass. The cold wine was delicious. She put the glass down and walked over to the bed, a little less steady on her high heels than she had been before.

Constantine was lying on his back. The girl with the smaller breasts was crouching over his face, and Corinda could clearly see the Greek's tongue lapping between her labia. The other girl had straddled his hips, just as Corinda had done minutes before with the prince. She was bouncing energetically on his cock, her round breasts wobbling and quivering. The chain that hung from the silver chokers around the girls' necks was swinging and jerking across Constantine's chest, their manacled wrists pulled together. Corinda saw the handle of one of the wooden phalluses sticking out from between his legs, the rest of it buried in his anus.

She knelt on the bed. She ran her hands up the front of both of the girls' bodies and cupped one of their breasts in each hand, comparing the two. She slipped her right hand down to the larger girl's clitoris, then leant forward and kissed her, slipping her tongue between her lips. The girl kissed back enthusiastically, her mouth hot and wet. Corinda felt her react as she butted her finger against her clit and fondled it gently. Her left hand was soon doing the same with the other girl, but this time she felt Constantine's tongue too, wiggling against her finger.

'Are you having a good time?' she asked him, breaking the kiss.

Seeing his cock embedded in the other girl provoked an odd emotion in her. Was it jealousy? Was it an overwhelming need to have her own sex filled despite the fact that she could still feel the shadow of the prince's cock inside her and feel his semen coating the walls of her vagina?

'Come on in, the water's fine,' Constantine said, moving his lips against the squatting girl's sex.

Corinda definitely wanted something inside her too. She saw the other wooden phallus lying on the bed and picked it up. Moving it between her legs she directed the tip of the carved shaft into her vagina. Without hesitation she pushed it inside herself. It was big, but the prince had opened her up and the sensation of being filled so completely delivered only raw pleasure.

Constantine wanted a change. He rolled the girl off his face and raised his head, watching Corinda tiddling the other girl's clit.

'Would you rather have the real thing?'

It was the second time a man had asked her that tonight.

'Oh yes.' The real thing would definitely be preferable.

The other girl pulled herself off Constantine's erection. She took the dildo between his legs and pulled it from his anus, making him gasp.

His eyes roamed over Corinda's body. They moved from her naked breasts to the stockings sheathing her legs, to her labia stretched around the girth of the wooden phallus. Getting up on his knees he came round behind her. He caressed her buttocks with both hands. The three strokes of the whip Dimitri had inflicted on her were still visible. He pushed his fingers under the stocking tops and caressed her flesh.

She could feel his wet, hard penis, pressed into the deep cleft of her buttocks. She wriggled against it. His hands left her stockings. One travelled to her breasts, cupping each in turn while the other pulled the dildo out of her sex and threw it aside. He pulled back so his cock nestled against her pussy. Despite her orgasms she felt a renewed stab of desire. Her body wanted more. She wanted more. She loved it. She loved men with throbbing cocks so eager to fill and fuck her.

'Yes,' she said, thrusting back on his cock.

'No!' The voice was like thunder. The prince stood at the side of the bed, his erection restored. In his mind Corinda was already his property, and she would be allowed no other men from now on.

Constantine understood at once. The deal was done. He had no regrets. He would get a good price for the girl, he knew that now. That was the main thing. He'd had his fun with her. He pulled away and rolled onto his back. The prince gestured to the two girls, who immediately scrambled to where Constantine lay. The larger one took his cock deep into her throat, while the other burrowed down between his thighs until she could get his balls into her mouth. She kissed them gently, then sucked them between her lips, first one, then both. Constantine closed his eyes and moaned. He had little to complain about.

The prince knelt on the bed. He took Corinda's face in his hands and kissed her. He plunged his tongue between her lips and pressed his chest against her breasts, whilst working a hand down over her buttocks.

'On your back,' he said. His tone had changed. It was an order not a request, but Corinda was in no condition to notice the difference. Her sex was throbbing with need. Denied Constantine's cock she needed a replacement. She needed it more desperately than she would have believed possible. She slithered onto her back and opened her legs, bending them at the knee. A few days ago she would not have known what to do. Now she knew better how to take and give pleasure.

'Is this what you want?' she asked, raising her foot and rubbing the sleek toes against Samora's glans.

He fell on her, driving his cock into the depths of her sex. His power, the strength of his body as well as the hardness of his cock, made Corinda come almost instantly. It was an orgasm born in her mind, as much as her body, provoked and stimulated by everything going on around her, as well as the incredible feeling of the rigid cock hammering into her.

Her senses were overwhelmed. To her side the two girls cooperated on Constantine's cock, sliding their mouths together up and down his shaft, their lips almost touching. One of them fingered his balls while the other drove the wooden phallus into his anus again. Corinda heard him cry out as an arc of spunk splattered onto his belly.

She had never before seen an ejaculation. It tipped her towards a new peak, another wave of pleasure rocking through her body. When it released her, if only temporarily, she realised the girls had left Constantine and were kneeling beside her. She felt hands and lips caressing her mouth, ears and neck. She felt a hand circling the base of the prince's cock and fingers sliding into her anus. She came again, probed and penetrated and fucked more totally than she had ever been. Her head arched back and her body went rigid as he thrust ever deeper into her. She felt bare, stripped of her defences, every nerve in her body raw, the core of her invaded as she took a blissful battering from his cock.

He came for the second time. In her imagination she could see it happening, the semen erupting from his cock just as it had from Constantine's minutes before.

She slept. It was her body's answer to the extremes of passion. It needed to rest. She had rolled onto her side the moment he climbed off her, and dozed off.

When she awoke the girls had gone and she was alone on the bed. She could see Constantine in his velvet robe, and the prince, dressed in a white towelling robe, standing by the coffee table. They were both drinking champagne.

'When will you leave?' Constantine asked.

'First thing in the morning.'

'More champagne?'

The prince held out his glass and Constantine refilled it.

'You must be hungry. Shall we go down to eat?'

'Let us conclude our business first. She's still asleep.'

Corinda was too comfortable to move. She lay luxuriating in the little tremors and thrills of pleasure her body seemed prone to producing.

'You haven't named a price yet,' the prince said.

'Dimitri offered fifty. He is very keen.'

'Seventy-five.'

'What happened to double?'

'Eighty.'

'Ninety-five.'

There was a pause.

'There is going to be no comeback on this?'

'My dear fellow, you've had two from me already. Would I let you down? Like the others she is classified "missing presumed dead". You can check for yourself. There is no family. Everyone thinks she is dead.'

Corinda's heart turned to ice.

'You are a very lucky man, Constantine.'

'Luck has nothing to do with it, my friend.'

'The shipwreck...'

'That had nothing to do with luck. I thought you knew that. My transmitters send out false navigation signals. The ships are drawn to me like iron filings to a magnet. The channel to the north is seeded with steel girders set in concrete. That's why my friends must always approach from the south.'

'So that's how it is done.'

'The modern equivalent of the old ship-wreckers, setting up a false lighthouse.'

'Well, it certainly brought you a special prize this time.'

'She belongs to you now, if we are agreed on ninety-three.'

'Agreed.'

'Good, good.' They shook hands.

Corinda felt a cold sweat break out on her forehead. She'd never imagined Constantine was responsible for the sinking. Suddenly everything was clear. The other men had come to the island to bid for her, to compete to see who would pay the highest price. She was chattel: an object to be bought and sold. And the prince had paid the most.

She shuddered to think what he would do to her when he got her to his country. Her mind was racing. What would be her fate? She imagined being locked in a seraglio with his other slaves, and made to serve him whenever he chose. She would rather die.

The prince noticed her eyes open.

'She's awake,' he hissed to Constantine, moving to the side of the bed. 'An exhausting experience,' he said, extending his hand to help her to her feet. 'I'm sure you would like to eat now.'

'Yes, that would be lovely,' she said. If they suspected she had overheard they might lock her away until the prince was ready to sail. She had to convince them she was still innocent of their intentions. It was her only chance of escape. And she had to escape.

She got up off the bed and stroked Samora's cheek affectionately. 'Aren't you exhausted? So much energy.' She ran her hand down to the front of the robe and rubbed his cock.

'I'm hungry, actually,' he said in his perfect English.

'Mmm... I could eat a horse,' she purred, giving his penis a suggestive squeeze.

'I don't think there's going to be time for that,' Constantine said to her, rather sternly. 'Take a shower in my bathroom. There's a robe in there for you.'

Corinda smiled as sincerely as she could. 'Won't be long,' she said, sidling towards the en-suite.

Chapter Nine

An extensive buffet had been laid out on the oak table in the dining room. There were plates filled with oysters, prawns and lobsters, a dish of caviar resting in ice, salads of fennel and red peppers, avocado and feta cheese, and four or five types of thinly cut salami and a whole honey-roasted ham, all arranged on a white linen cloth. The two slave girls, now demurely dressed in shapeless maroon dresses, though still tethered by the chains at their necks and wrists, had already helped themselves by the time Constantine and the prince led Corinda into the room.

She pretended to be hungry but ate little. She had put on the towelling robe in the bathroom, as Constantine had suggested, and let down her long blonde hair.

The prince kept complimenting her on how beautiful she looked, and ran his hands down her back and over her pert buttocks. For her part she tried to respond with smiles and an expression that suggested she found him the most fascinating man in the world, with no hint, she hoped, that she knew what he had planned for her.

'Well,' he said, after devouring a large quantity of caviar, 'I hope you'll find my yacht comfortable.'

'I'll be glad of the fresh air,' she said.

'Of course. I'm sure we'll have a lot of fun.'

She wondered how and when he would break the news that their destination was not England, and how he planned to restrain her from then on. Or did he imagine she would go quietly, a willing slave to the handsome prince? She shuddered at the thought.

'Are you cold, my dear?' Constantine asked, spotting her reaction.

'I'm tired, I think. If you'll forgive me I'd like to get an early night. I want to be at my best tomorrow.'

'Naturally,' the prince said sympathetically. He stroked her cheek and kissed her fleetingly on the lips. 'Get some rest.'

'Will I see you in the morning?' she asked Constantine.

'Oh yes. We will say goodbye then.' He smiled at her, his gold teeth catching the light.

'I'll be quite sad,' she said, touching his arm. It was a good performance, she thought. She wanted to choke on every word but she managed to make her eyes sparkle with a look of gratitude.

Iluska was summoned to show her back to her room. The brunette led her through the dining room and into the atrium. As soon as she was out of sight of the men Corinda started to look around. She had barely taken any interest in the geography of the house before she had realised her predicament. Now she was looking for a means of escape.

'How do you get outside?' she asked the Albanian.

'Is forbidden,' was the tart reply.

As they got to the corridor that led to her room Corinda noticed a porcelain vase on a stand by the wall. It was filled with a huge display of orange flowers. She could have used it to hit the brunette over the head and knock her out. But that was no good. They would soon discover her and raise the alarm before she had found a way out of the building.

They reached the entrance to her room. The girl operated the switch and the shutter rolled up. As Corinda walked inside she could see Iluska waited in the corridor until the shutter had completely closed again.

What on earth was she going to do? She had to escape, but how? She had no idea how long it would be before they came to get her but she had to find a way out by then. Quickly she pulled the robe off. She rifled through the wardrobe and found a plain brown cotton shift. It was practical and would be difficult to spot in the dark. She decided against shoes. There were no flat heels in the collection and the high heels would slow her down.

The next problem was how to open the metal shutter. She debated about waiting until everyone had gone to bed before doing anything, but decided that would not only give her less time to find a way out, but that the noise of the shutter rolling open would be even more noticeable in the dead of night. Her best chance of it not being heard was now, with Constantine and the prince in the dining room.

But that didn't solve the problem of how to open it. She tried to remember exactly what Eloisa had done this morning. She certainly wasn't carrying any remote control that would account for the door opening so conveniently at exactly the right moment. There must be something in the room itself, a hidden switch of some sort. Where had she stood? Corinda moved to the foot of the bed, as near as possible to where she thought Eloisa had been, then dropped to her knees to examine the floor. As far as she could see there was nothing; the carpeting was as smooth and flat as in any other part of the room. There was nothing on the leg of the bed either. How could she have opened the shutter?

She sat on the floor with her legs crossed. Arabella had given her a good grounding in all the modern sciences including electronics and computers. She tried to remember any other ways an electronic circuit could be activated. There were light sensitive diodes, but she couldn't see how that would work in this room. There were sound sensitive circuits too. Sound. That made sense; a switch triggered by a certain sound.

On most occasions, when she'd been brought breakfast, the shutter had remained open. But on those few occasions when Eloisa had remained in the room with her the American had said something when they were ready to leave. 'Ready,' she said loudly. Nothing happened. That wasn't it. She'd said something else. 'We're off,' she tried. Again nothing. It was something like that. 'Come on,' she said. That wasn't it. 'Let's go,' she said. Immediately the roller mechanism began to grind. She'd done it! *Go* was the key word.

As soon as the metal shutter had rolled up a foot or two she squeezed under it and hit the switch on the corridor wall to keep the noise to a minimum. It descended again and hit the floor with a clunk Corinda swore would have woken the dead. Standing stock still she listened for any sound that might indicate someone had been disturbed by the noise. None came. Very faintly she thought she could hear voices. Voices, coming from the dining room.

Getting out of her room was the least of her problems. Now she had to get out of the house. There must be an exit and logically it would be on the ground floor. That meant going back towards the dining room to search, as she was sure none of the metal shutters in the corridor led to anything but other bedrooms.

As quietly as she could she tiptoed down the passageway and into the atrium with its false glass ceiling, of stars sparkling in a night sky. She worked her way around the walls, to a small door she had noticed under the staircase. Other than the arched entrance to the main reception room, it was the only door on the ground floor. The noise of the voices was louder. At any moment she expected the prince or Constantine to stride out of the dining room and find her.

She turned the handle of the door. It opened inward. She crept inside then closed the door with infinite care. She was in a long narrow passage with several doors on either side. Clinging to the wall she inched her way along. There was much more noise here. She heard voices, male and female, and the noise of crockery and cutlery being washed up. She was passing the kitchens. Again she held her breath, expecting one of the doors to burst open at any second.

They didn't. The passage opened into a wider space at the far end, with two doors. She had no choice but to try one of them, despite the fact she had no idea where they might lead. It was quite possible they opened into the dining room and she would be caught immediately.

Tentatively she eased the nearest one open and glanced inside. It was a storage cupboard lined with shelves of kitchen supplies. She closed it quietly and tried the second. It was much heavier. Her heart was in her mouth as she pulled it back. She expected the worst, but she was safe. Beyond lay another corridor. It was floored with dark brown marble, and modern tapestries in bright colours hung from the walls. There were two large doors on either side, but the most bizarre feature was the narrow opening at the far end. It was not fitted with a door but instead appeared to be filled with a dense black material. As she tiptoed closer she saw it was not material at all, but long black nylon fibres extending from the walls and ceiling of another passageway. The fibres intersected at the centre. Hanging from hooks to one side of the entrance were several red facemasks, with transparent windows for eyes.

Corinda's heart beat faster. This was the exit. The fibres had been designed to prevent any light entering from the outside as an exterior door was opened, the masks available to protect the face. She was sure that was the only explanation. Quickly she hooked a mask over her face, took a depth breath and plunged forward into the tightly packed fibres. They pricked at her body. She forced her way forward. It was hard going. As the fibres in front of her parted the ones behind folded back into place behind her, until she was completely engulfed by them. She fought the feeling of claustrophobia and panic and pressed forward. The blackness was as total as the darkness in her bedroom. The fibres made every movement an effort, like walking in thick mud. It was even difficult to breath.

She found it was easier if she walked sideways, offering less resistance to the matted nylon. She pushed and wriggled, sweat breaking out on her body. At last she felt the fibres parting and almost fell over as her forward momentum met no resistance and she plunged out of the darkness into the light. She found herself in a small space lined with what looked like black rubber, the light coming from a small electric lamp overhead. In front of her was a perfectly normal door, secured on the inside with two steel bolts. She hung the mask up with several others and unbolted the door. Closing it quietly, she found herself in yet another passage, also lined with black rubber and faintly lit from above. It was no more than six feet long and there was another bolted door at the end.

She knew before she opened it that this door led outside. She could smell fresh air. The outer door was surrounded by heavy rubber seals. She unbolted it and took hold of the steel handle. She pulled and felt the hydraulic hinges moving. The door gapped open.

She could never remember getting a bigger shock. Instead of the darkness of night she had expected bright sunlight flooded the passage, momentarily blinding her with its intensity. Eventually she lowered her hands and screwed her eyes against the harsh glare.

It was midday, the sun high in the sort of blue sky Corinda had spent much of her childhood playing under on her own island. The outer door was at the bottom of a steep concrete ramp below ground level. Trying to get over the total disorientation she felt, and shielding her eyes against the sun with her hand, she ran up the ramp. Trees and vegetation surrounded the house. There was a cluster of palms just the other side of the dirt track at the top of the ramp. She raced across into it, not stopping until she was well hidden in its undergrowth. Then she dropped to her knees, her heart thumping and her breath short.

She looked back at the house. It was ugly and squat, most of it buried below ground level, its concrete walls painted a mottled dark green, like camouflage. It was approached by the dirt track which had been cut through the vegetation growing unchecked everywhere else; in many places it tenaciously climbed the walls of the house. Beyond she could see a beach and the rolling sea. As far as she could tell there was only the single exit through which she had escaped.

She tried to orientate herself in time. She remembered Constantine had said he went out at night. Presumably he had shifted time in the lightless house, so night became day for him. He slept while the sun was out, and roamed the island at night.

Not that this speculation helped her. She had, for the moment, escaped his clutches. But if the island was small and uninhabited, as he'd said, it would not be long before she was recaptured.

The first thing she had to do was establish how big the island was and if there were any other people on it. Constantine had lied about everything else and it was quite possible he had lied about that. From where she was she could only see the shoreline reaching out to her left. The house was situated on a small headland and obstructed the view on the other side where, presumably, the prince's yacht was moored. The only way to find out how large the island was, she reasoned, would be by following the shoreline. If there were other people they would have boats, or other means of contacting the outside world.

Still finding it hard to accept it was not the middle of the night, she moved through the trees. Fortunately the outline of the forest ran along the beach so she could follow the shore without being too conspicuous. One good thing about her escape was that she didn't imagine anyone would check her room until what passed for morning in the house.

It was hot. The dark cotton dress was soaked with perspiration. She would have liked to throw herself into the sea, the gentle waves lapping at the white crystal sand, but dare not for fear of being seen or wasting precious time.

She walked miles without seeing anything that might suggest other inhabitants. There were no footsteps in the sand, no little rowing boats or makeshift jetties, and no litter. She could still see the headland where Constantine's house was sited, but the house itself had merged into the background.

The sun had begun to sink towards the horizon, though it was a long way from dipping below it, when she saw a small stream that ran into the sea. It cut through the trees, and she got some relief from the heat by wading into its cool waters.

It was then that she saw it. The sun glinted from a pane of glass. It was not easy to make it out at first, but as she walked up onto a small rise, on the other side of the stream she saw a large square house set in a copse of trees. It was surrounded on all sides by a tall wooden fence, largely overgrown with climbing shrubs. Unlike the house she had just left there were large windows, most of which, she noticed, were barred.

Her hopes were raised. She wanted to rush forward but instinct made her more circumspect. She approached the house cautiously, keeping well down. A dirt track had been cut through the forest at the back of the house, where the fencing enclosed a little courtyard. It was a good thing she trusted her instincts; as she stopped to look more closely a figure appeared in one of the downstairs windows. It was Eloisa.

'Over here,' Eloisa said. She tapped the tip of the whip against a narrow bench with a slatted surface. It was bolted to the floor.

Tim Morrison was kneeling on the floor in front of her, his eyes lowered. He had learnt from bitter experience over the last few days that if he did not adopt the position when she entered the room it would be the worst for him. He had learnt to obey all her orders without question. The price of disobedience was too high.

Quickly he scrambled to his feet. He was naked apart from leather cuffs strapped around his wrists and ankles.

'On your back,' Eloisa ordered.

He lay on the bench. It was just wide enough to accommodate his body.

'Hands above your head.'

Again he obeyed. Eloisa was wearing black high-heeled boots, a black leather bra, and leather shorts that fitted her like a second skin. Pulling his wrists up in turn she fastened snap-hooks, attached to the legs of the bench, into D-rings on the cuffs. She walked to the foot of the bench, trailing the whip along his naked body, and soon had his ankles secured in the same way. There was a broad leather belt attached to the middle of the bench, which she wrapped around his waist and buckled tight. Her victim was helpless.

She stood looking down at him, enjoying the sense of power she had over him. He belonged to her. He could be made to do anything she required. Anything. The idea made her body throb with sexual pleasure. Of course her preference was for women, and she had used many in this room over her years with Constantine, but she was not averse to an occasional man, as she had proved with Yves. And like the Frenchman, Tim Morrison was a fine specimen. She had greatly enjoyed training him to her special needs over the last few days.

'That's better, isn't it?' she said.

She stood by his head so he was staring up her thighs to her crotch, where the leather shorts covered her sex so tightly. She saw his cock beginning to stir and flicked it with the tip of the riding crop.

'I haven't told you about your little friend, have I?'

His penis was unfurling rapidly. 'What have you done to her?'

'Nothing she wasn't only too willing to try, I assure you.'

'You bitch,' he hissed.

Thwack! The whip landed across his thighs, narrowly missing his balls.

'I would be very careful if I were you. You are in no position to hurl insults.'

Eloisa unzipped the leather shorts and drew them slowly down her long legs and over her boots. She unclipped the leather bra, releasing her breasts, then cupped them in her hands, playing with her stiff nipples.

'We'll start with something simple, shall we?' she said. She raised her left leg and straddled the bench so her groin was poised directly above his face and she was looking down into his eyes. He stared up into her pouting sex, the lips moistening with anticipation.

Eloisa stroked between them. 'You're going to give me a good licking. Just like your little friend did.' She lowered herself down until her sex was an inch from his mouth. 'Come on,' she prompted, lashing out with the whip behind her back and catching him a glancing blow on his stomach.

He strained his head up off the bench to reach her, his shoulders already cramped by his bondage. He managed to get his tongue into her sex. With no support his neck muscles ached. But he tried to ignore them and hold his position, as his tongue found and stroked the American's swollen clitoris.

'Harder,' Eloisa complained, flicking him with the whip again. But to his relief she allowed herself to sink lower so he could rest his head back on the slatted wooden bench. He concentrated on circling her clit with his tongue, as she had taught him she liked. He heard her moan and felt her shudder. 'So good,' she urged, stroking his blond hair. 'Perhaps I will keep you here. Constantine usually sells the men to the Arabs, but in your case it would be such a waste. I could keep you as my slave. You'd like that, wouldn't you?'

He tried to nod without breaking his rhythm, not wanting to antagonise her further.

Eloisa leant back until she could rest her hands on his thighs, so her body was stretched back over him and her labia was thrust more forcibly against his mouth. His tongue slipped into her vagina and her clitoris ground against his nose. She felt her orgasm exploding. She could have held it back but there was no need. It would only be the first of many. He was there to be used; her slave, her victim. It was that thought that made her come so quickly.

'Yesss,' she hissed, closing her eyes, letting the feelings wash over her. 'I'm going to let you fuck me today,' she said. 'A special privilege.' She didn't move, waiting for the initial pleasure to subside.

Slowly she got to her feet. His mouth and chin were wet with her juices. She wiped them with her hand, then licked her fingers and tasted herself eagerly. She lifted her leg and straddled the bench again, this time with her thighs either side of his hips. His erection was pulsing, the glans perfectly smooth. She took it in her hand and squeezed, then slapped it with her palm. Gradually she bent her knees and lowered herself onto it, guiding it between her labia with her fingers, her eyes staring into his. She nudged the tip against her clit and was hit by a wave of sensation so intense it forced her eyes closed.

Corinda timed her moment perfectly. There was a small glass panel in the door, and though Eloisa's back was to her the shudder of pleasure was unmistakable. She dashed in and struck Eloisa over the head with a branch she'd picked up outside. The American pitched forward heavily, then rolled to the floor.

Seeing Tim had been the second shock of the day. 'You're alive,' she said. 'Oh God, you're alive!' She hugged his chest. 'Oh thank God, you're alive.' She had seen him through the window as she approached the house and could hardly believe her eyes. She'd seen what Eloisa was doing too, and knew she had to rescue him.

Eloisa moaned and rolled onto her side.

'Quick,' Tim said, 'get me up.'

Corinda unsnapped the hooks that bound him to the bench and unbuckled the leather belt around his waist. Rubbing his arms and shoulders he got to his feet.

'We've got to tie her up,' he said quickly.

There was a length of rope hanging from a pulley that was hooked into a beam running across the ceiling. The American had already used it to string him up. Pulling it from the metal block he rolled Eloisa onto her stomach, and before she had begun to recover her senses bound her wrists together. He forced her legs back, and tied her ankles too. Then he bound them to her wrists, so she was hogtied and helpless.

'Gag her,' he said as he completed the job. Corinda picked up the leather bra. She stuffed it into Eloisa's mouth then used the belt from the leather shorts to tie it in place, just as Eloisa's eyes opened. She realised what they had done to her and began to struggle. Fortunately she could do no more than rock from side to side. She tried to scream for help but could produce only a muffled moan.

'How did you get here?' Tim asked.

'This way,' she said, taking his hand. She wanted to kiss him and hug him, but there was no time. They ran down the short corridor outside his cell. It opened into the courtyard at the back of the building. Lying by the gate in the fence was a man in a shabby grey uniform. He too had fallen victim to Corinda's hefty wooden branch, and lay in the dirt breathing heavily.

Tim dropped to his side.

'What are you doing?' Corinda said.

Tim unzipped the man's trousers and began pulling them off his legs.

'There's no time,' Corinda said.

'I've got to wear something.' He pulled one leg free, then the other, then quickly pulled the trousers on. They were too big for him. He pulled the man's watch off his wrist and strapped it on his own. 'We've got to tie him up too,' he said as the man began to come round.

'No time. Quick.'

Corinda caught his hand again and pulled him out into the forest, running as fast as she could.

'What are we going to do?' Tim panted.

'We've got to find a boat. It's the only way off the island. Constantine is mad.'

'I know that.'

'There might be a jetty on the other side of the headland,' Corinda said, their progress slowed by the thick foliage.

'There is. I saw it when they brought me here.'

'You were in the other house?' She looked astonished. 'Constantine told me he didn't know what had happened to you.'

'No, no. They boarded the yacht and ransacked it. I managed to get us into a life-raft. They ran it down.'

'My God.'

'I saw at least two motorboats tied up at the jetty. If we can get one of them out to sea we'll hopefully be picked up by a passing yacht.'

Corinda stopped for a moment. 'It's so good to see you,' she said, looking into his face. She felt tears well up in her eyes.

'It's good to see you, too. I had no idea what they were doing to you.'

They fought on through the heavy undergrowth, following the direct track but not daring to use it. It was just as well. Twenty or so minutes into their trek an open Land Rover came careering down the road towards the beach house. Minutes later they heard its engine returning. It drove by slowly, Eloisa and two guards mounted in the back, staring into the forest for any sign of life. Tim and Corinda threw themselves to the ground and did not move again until the noise of the engine had faded completely.

'Damn,' Tim said. 'They're bound to guard the boats now.'

'Are you a good swimmer?' Corinda asked as they pressed forward again.

'Yes. Why?'

She explained about the prince's yacht. It would not be moored on the jetty, she suspected. It would be anchored some way off. It might have a motorboat they could take.

'Good idea,' Tim agreed.

They slowed their pace, wanting to conserve their energy. It was dark by the time they saw the lights in the distance. The last mile they had been forced to walk on the track because the forest had become too dense. All the time they kept their ears open for any engines. Nothing had come along. It would be obvious to Constantine that the only means of escape were the boats on the jetty, so he was concentrating his forces there.

As soon as they saw the lights they ran under cover again. Fortunately there was a line of shrubs running right down to the beach. They moved through them as stealthily as possible until they could get a good look at the jetty. There were two large motorboats moored to it, with a guard sitting in each and another two standing by the mooring capstans. Eloisa strode up and down the wooden planks, her anger obvious from her strutting steps. There was no way they would be able to overpower the five of them.

'There,' Corinda whispered, pointing out to sea.

Anchored in the natural bay formed by the headland on one side and a sweeping outcrop of rocks on the other, was a three-masted yacht, with several lights hanging from the rigging. But as far as they could see there was no smaller boat moored next to it.

'No boat,' Tim whispered.

'It'll be on the other side,' Corinda said.

They heard an engine start. The battered Land Rover, with headlights blazing, rattled down to the jetty. The prince and Constantine stepped out.

They were close enough to hear their voices as they talked to Eloisa.

'Have you seen them?' Constantine snapped.

'No, but don't worry. They won't get off the island.'

'This is all your fault,' the prince accused Constantine. 'All your ridiculous pretence. I should have taken her aboard straight away.'

'You didn't object at the time,' Constantine snapped back.

'Just find her,' Samora replied, getting into the back of the vehicle.

'Keep us informed,' Constantine told Eloisa, before getting back into the front seat and driving off.

'Look,' Corinda whispered to Tim, 'I'm a good swimmer. I can swim out there and back with no trouble. The sea's calm. If there's a boat on the other side I'll steal it. The problem is, if they hear the sound of a motorboat engine they'll immediately follow it. We've got to disable these boats first.'

'We could just drift.'

'Too risky. We wouldn't get far. If someone on the yacht notices the boat gone they could find us in minutes with these motorboats.'

Tim thought for a minute. 'I've got it. How long will it take you to swim out there? About thirty minutes, and thirty minutes back, right?'

'Yes.'

'So if you're not back on the beach here in an hour I'll know there is a boat, right?'

'Yes.'

'Good. If there isn't one you'll swim back and we'll have to think again. But if there is don't start the engine until you see my signal after the hour is up. Then come in and pick me up. I'll make sure we can't be chased. I've got the watch to time you.' He indicated the guard's watch on his wrist.

'What are you going to do?'

'They won't be in any state to chase us,' he said, grinning.

'All right. Be careful, Tim,' she said, touching his cheek.

'You too.'

She slipped off her dress. Despite the circumstances she saw him looking at her naked body.

Very quietly she scurried across the beach and waded into the water. She swam slowly to avoid causing any disturbance, but further out, with the risk of being seen diminished, she began to swim more powerfully. Stretching out she was glad to be using her muscles again, and even gladder to be swimming away from the island, if only temporarily. As she got into her stride, kicking her legs and bringing her arms over to cut into the water in a perfectly executed front crawl, she began to think of Tim. Her relief at seeing him alive again was only tempered by their present situation. She had seen what Eloisa was doing to him and wondered what else he had been made to suffer at her hands.

The yacht loomed nearer and she swam more slowly again, so she would not be seen if anyone was on deck. She headed for the stern, then slowly rounded it, almost not bearing to see at what lay on the other side. But she had been right. As she swam she saw the outline of a sleek motorboat, moored to a gangplank on the other side of the yacht.

Going very gently she swam to it. As far as she could tell there was no one on deck. She pulled herself out of the water and into the motorboat. Another piece of luck. The keys were in the ignition, the crew obviously expecting no thieves on a private island. There was a clock too, showing it had taken her exactly twenty-four minutes to swim from the beach. It was ten minutes past six.

The time passed slowly. Her mind drifted. She thought of what the prince had done to her last night, and how it had made her feel. The fact of Constantine's betrayal did not change the way she felt about men or about sex. She ached to have a man again, but this time, hopefully, it would be Tim. They would be able to finish what they had started on the yacht a few days ago.

It was six thirty-five. Occasionally she heard movement on the yacht, but it was distant. She could hear a radio playing Glen Miller. Six thirty-six. She couldn't see the jetty from here, only the outline of the strange concrete house, silhouetted against the dark sky by a near full moon that played hide and seek with drifting clouds. If they escaped they would lead the police back here and no doubt, literally as well as metaphorically, bring new light to bear on Constantine's nefarious business.

Six thirty-seven. Corinda heard a new sound. It was the engine of the Land Rover. But it was not chugging along gently as it had done before. It was racing. That was the signal, she knew at once. She turned the ignition of the motorboat's engine and it growled into life. Fortunately she knew how to handle it. In fact she was expert, taught by the woman who had been employed to teach her to water-ski.

She swept the boat around the yacht in a wide arc and headed for the jetty. The noise roused the men aboard, who rushed up on deck. But there was nothing they could do but stand and stare. Corinda could see the Land Rover now. It was powering down the road from the house at full speed. Eloisa and the guards had seen it too and were standing still, watching it approach. As it got nearer to them it did not slow, but accelerated, careering directly towards the jetty. It was obvious what it was going to do so Eloisa and the men around her jumped out of the way. The Land Rover mounted the jetty, heading for the two boats. It veered sharply to the right and plunged into the sea, right on top of them. At the very last moment Corinda saw a shadowy figure jump clear.

She opened the throttle and gunned the engine, sweeping towards the wreckage. Both boats had been smashed, but in the inky-black water there was no sign of Tim.

'Oh God,' she said aloud, cutting the engines to listen for him. The water was slicked with oil and she heard a muffled explosion followed by the flicker of fire. In seconds the whole jetty was alight and the flames were heading across the water towards her boat.

'Here!' Tim screamed. He had surfaced ten yards away in the middle of the oil. She throttled forward and turned the wheel, so the boat would travel in a sweeping curve towards him. As it approached he threw his arm over the side.

'Go, go, go!' he shouted. The flames licked at his feet as he pulled himself aboard. The engine accelerated, and the bow of the boat rose up as the big propellers bit deeply into the water. The boat surged forward at full speed, heading for the open sea.

Chapter Ten

'Look!' exclaimed Corinda excitedly.

A red light and a green light bobbed up and down high above the water.

'It's definitely a yacht,' Tim said. 'And a big one.'

They had run out of fuel half an hour before, though they were well clear of the island. The clouds had gathered, totally obscuring the moon, and it was very dark. The clock on the instrument panel told them it was one o'clock in the morning.

They approached the anchored yacht slowly, with nothing but the drift of the current to move them. There was no sign of anyone aboard, the crew, presumably all asleep. As they nudged against the side of the sleek white boat Tim grabbed the anchor cable and tied a line to it.

'We'll have to wait until morning,' he said. 'It's too high to climb the sides.'

'We could bang on them,' Corinda suggested.

'No need to do that.'

The voice came from above them. It was English. A thin shadow looked down over the side of the yacht. He held a torch, which he shone into the motorboat.

'Are you in trouble?' The torch beam played on Corinda's nakedness.

'We've run out of fuel,' Tim explained.

'Come aboard then. I'll lower the gangplank.'

The man disappeared. A minute or two later they heard the grinding of machinery. A floodlight lit the side of the yacht and they saw a steel structure being lowered from a gantry projecting over its side. It formed a staircase with a platform at the bottom. Tim untied the mooring and the motorboat drifted back along the hull until he could tie it to the steps.

Corinda went up first, the man waiting at the top to greet her.

'Malcolm Arlington,' he said, taking her hand to help her aboard. His eyes feasted on her voluptuous body, bathed in the stark floodlights.

'Corinda Chaste,' she said, showing no embarrassment at her nakedness. 'This is very good of you.'

'Not at all.'

As Tim climbed aboard a woman appeared from one of the cabins. She had dark olive skin, and black hair that reached almost to her waist. She was one of the most beautiful women Corinda had ever seen.

'Candy, darling, we have visitors,' Malcolm said.

'So I see,' she replied. She had clearly been roused from her sleep. She tied the sash of a cream satin robe around her body and walked towards them. She was wearing cream satin slippers with a white boa feather on each of the toes.

'We're really terribly sorry to disturb you,' Tim said.

'Did you have an accident?' Candy asked, shaking her hair out and looking, with one eyebrow raised, at Corinda's naked body.

'It's a long story,' Tim replied.

'Well, you were fortunate it's such a warm night. Come in. I'm sure you could use a drink.'

'Oh, yes please,' Corinda said. After six hours at sea she was thirsty.

'And I'll find you something to wear, or my husband's eyes will never go back into their sockets,' Candy said. Then turning to Tim she said, 'And you could obviously use something too.' He'd had to knot the guard's grey trousers around his waist to keep them up, and they were too short for his long legs.

Malcolm led the way into the main stateroom. The yacht was every bit as luxurious as the Chaste yacht had been. The stateroom was decorated in cream and beige, with roman blinds at the windows and a large beige banquette built out from two of the walls. There was a bar, complete with chrome and leather stools. Halogen lights concealed in the ceiling gave the room a pleasant, warm glow.

'What will you have?' Malcolm asked.

'Brandy, please,' Corinda said. She sat on the banquette. 'But I'd like some water too.'

Malcolm looked at Tim.

'The same,' he said. 'This really is very kind of you.'

He handed them two glasses of sparkling mineral water, which they drank thirstily, then poured large measures of Camus XO into glasses the size of melons, and left them on the coffee table in front of them. He poured two more brandies, leaving one on the bar and taking his own over to the banquette where he sat next to Corinda. 'Cheers,' he said, looking blatantly at her breasts.

'Thank you,' Corinda said, sipping the brandy.

'I hope you don't mind me saying so... Corinda, is it? But you are a very beautiful young woman.'

'Yes, she certainly is.' There was a spiral staircase at the back of the stateroom leading to the upper and lower decks. It was made from tubular chromium steel with ash steps. Candy spoke as she came down it. 'Very beautiful,' she agreed.

She dropped a T-shirt and a pair of shorts in front of Tim, and handed Corinda a black lace nightgown. 'I think you and I are about the same size,' she said, looking at Corinda's body as avariciously as her husband was. She took the remaining brandy balloon from the bar and downed half of it with a single gulp.

Corinda stood up. She pulled the nightgown over her head and let the soft silk drop around her body. The gown had two diagonal inserts of lace positioned so that they revealed a great deal of breast and tummy, and her downy pubis. It only served to increase the allure of her body.

'Mmm... it's so soft,' she said, stroking the material on her thigh.

'Is there anywhere I could change?' Tim asked.

'Of course, there's a cloakroom,' Malcolm said, indicating a small wooden door to the side of the spiral staircase.

'Thanks,' he said, hastily picking up the clothes and disappearing inside.

'That suits you,' Malcolm said.

'Do you think so?' Corinda twirled around. 'Your husband's really very attractive,' she said. 'I'd love to have sex with him.'

Candy laughed. 'Well, you get right to the point, don't you?'

'Am I wrong to say that?' Corinda asked anxiously. 'I'm sorry if that's embarrassing. I'm afraid I'm not very up on social etiquette, especially when it comes to sex.'

'I'm very flattered,' Malcolm said, winking at his wife.

'But have I offended you?'

'Not at all. It's nice to find someone so open on the subject of sex. Most people play games and never come out with the truth.'

'Tim told me about that,' Corinda said. 'I think it's a bit silly.'

'He's obviously not so broadminded,' Candy said.

Tim walked out of the cloakroom. 'What's that?' he asked.

'I was telling Malcolm, I would really like to have sex with him,' Corinda explained.

Tim gulped. 'What?'

'Your friend appears to be very uninhibited in expressing her feelings,' Candy said. She sat in a cone-shaped armchair and crossed her legs. The white satin of her robe fell away to reveal an expanse of tanned, slender thigh.

'I must apologise. The thing is she's had a rather unusual upbringing.'

'They didn't mind, Tim. I told you it's better to be honest about these things,' she said.

'So what brings you out here in the middle of the night, with no fuel and no clothes?' Malcolm asked.

Tim sat down again. 'It really is a long story.'

'Please, we're fascinated,' Candy said.

They shared the telling. Tim told them about the Chaste legacy, Corinda about her education on the island and the shipwreck, and Tim concluded with the story of how they had both been kept prisoner on the island, leaving out his treatment at the hands of Eloisa.

'Where do you want to go, incidentally?' Malcolm asked.

'Well ultimately London, but if you could drop us off at the nearest port...' Tim replied.

'Don't be silly.' He looked directly at his wife. 'We're heading for Southampton. You're quite welcome to hitch a lift. No problem is it, darling?'

'No problem,' Candy agreed, getting to her feet. 'I think you'd probably like to get some sleep after all your adventures. Come on, Malcolm, let's show them to a nice comfortable cabin.'

'Absolutely,' he said. 'This way.' He smiled at his wife and their eyes met in a meaningful look.

Candy led the way down the spiral stairs and along a narrow companionway, the walls of which were lined with panels of highly varnished light oak, set in brass. She opened one of the small doors.

'There's a bathroom, and there should be towels and everything you need. Sleep well,' she said.

'Yes,' Malcolm added. 'Just relax, and don't worry about a thing.'

The couple headed back the way they had come, leaving Tim and Corinda to file into the bedroom. It was not large but well appointed, with a double bed facing two built-in wardrobes in the middle of which was a vanity unit. On a shelf above this was a television. The wardrobes and the walls of the room were lined with pale varnished sycamore, and the counterpane of the bed was a green and black tartan. The carpet too was dark green.

Corinda gazed out of one of the brass portholes, but could see nothing but a few stars. 'We've really hit lucky,' she said.

'They seem like a nice couple,' Tim agreed.

'Very nice. He's almost as handsome as you.' They took turns to shower in the small bathroom, Tim allowing Corinda to go first. She had pulled back the counterpane on the bed and was lying naked across the white linen sheets by the time he finished and came back into the bedroom with a towel wrapped

114

around his waist.

'Are you too tired?' Corinda asked.

'Too tired for what?' he said.

'Too tired to ravish me,' she replied. She got up on her knees and grabbed a corner of the towel, pulling it away from his hips. 'I've learnt a lot since we were last together.'

'Have you? I feared the worst.' He looked concerned.

'Oh, don't worry.' She dropped the towel on the floor and cupped her breasts in her hands. 'If you want the truth, I enjoy it. I had no idea sex could be so interesting. I've made my mind up to have a lot of it.'

'Did you?' Tim was experiencing the same dilemma he had suffered on the yacht a week earlier. The girl had been his responsibility, his charge, for the last year since his father had died. He shouldn't really be responding to her sexually. But he found it impossible to resist her. She was making his penis harden rapidly.

'Oh yes. I learnt what men like, Tim. Do you like black stockings, for instance? Shiny, sheer black stockings? Do you like taut black suspenders and high-heeled shoes? Can you imagine what I look like in them?'

'Yes,' he said, hardly able to form the word, his mouth dry.

'Look, you've got an erection already and I haven't even touched you,' she said, pointing at his penis, now almost vertical.

'I told you before, Corinda, I'm not sure we should be doing this.'

'Don't you want me to suck it?' She scrambled across the bed and licked the tip of his glans.

'Corinda!' he protested. But he didn't have the strength to pull away as her lips closed over his cock.

'She's so enthusiastic.'

'And so sexy.'

Malcolm was lying back on the double bed in the master bedroom. Opposite the bed, built into the wall, was a large television screen.

'Oh, my God, you really have learnt about sex, haven't you?' Tim said.

His voice was tinny, the hidden microphone small and producing too much treble. Malcolm decided he must get it changed for a better model. But the picture was crystal clear. The video camera was concealed in the television above the vanity unit, and he could see Corinda's cheeks dimpling as she sucked Tim's cock, her breasts swinging gently as she leant forward.

'I wonder what she's like with a woman,' Candy said. She was standing by the side of the bed, brushing her long black hair. She had stripped off her robe and was naked. Her body was slender as a result of a carefully controlled diet and regular exercise. Her legs were shapely, her breasts round and firm, with large areolae and dark nipples. Her belly was flat and her mons was covered with thick black hair.

'You can't wait to get your hands on her, can you?' he said.

'Come on, you can do better than that,' Candy scolded. 'Not so fast.'

On either side of her husband were two girls; a short-haired blonde and a redhead. Both wore red leather corsets laced at the back, with quarter-cup bras that left their breasts exposed. They each wore a red leather collar and cuffs around their wrists. The cuffs were chained to a ring in front of the collar making them hold their hands up under their chins. The redhead was kneeling with her head bobbing up and down in Malcolm's lap, his cock deep in her mouth.

Candy slapped her buttocks with the palm of her hand. The girl slowed her movements, taking longer to work her mouth up and down.

'Oh Tim, you feel so good.' Corinda had pulled her mouth from Tim's cock and straightened up. She kissed him, her lips crushing against his. 'Please fuck me,' she said breathlessly. 'Please, I've thought about it so much.'

They watched as Corinda slid back on to the bed. She opened her legs and arched her buttocks, angling her sex up at Tim. The camera picked up every detail. They could see her labia as they opened to reveal the pink nub of her clitoris and the scarlet wetness of her vagina.

'Look at that,' Malcolm said. 'The little bitch is begging for it.'

Candy propped a pillow against the padded headboard and lay on the bed next to the blonde. She spread her legs apart to reveal the dark thatch of her pubic hair. 'Come on,' she said, 'get your head down.'

Awkwardly, with her hands tied to her neck, the girl slithered down the bed. Lying on her stomach she wriggled until her mouth was within range of Candy's sex. She extended her tongue and parted the thick black hair, searching for her clitoris.

'Mmm...' Candy shuddered as the girl's tongue found its target.

On the television screen Tim was on top of Corinda, as she lifted her legs and wrapped them around his back.

'Now I've got you,' her tinny voice said over the speaker. She squeezed her thighs. The tone of her voice changed. 'Oh Tim, that's what I've wanted...'

They could see him buck his hips. His cock parted her sex lips and slipped effortlessly into the depths of her vagina, disappearing completely.

'Use your fingers,' Candy ordered. The blonde between her legs manoeuvred one hand so she could push her fingers into the woman's sex.

'They're well trained,' Malcolm said, taking his eyes off the screen long enough to watch the blonde working on his wife.

'You're making me come,' Corinda said, attracting Malcolm's attention back to the screen.

Tim was powering his cock in and out of her. The little microphone picked up Corinda's moans of delight.

'I know,' Tim whispered into her ear. 'I can feel it.'

'Don't you wish you were giving it to her?' Candy said.

'Oh yes.'

'Do you want to come now?' Candy asked.

'Yes. This is a real turn on.'

'Come over my tits then.'

Malcolm got to his knees, pushed the redhead away and worked himself around so his cock was over his wife's breasts. The girl's saliva had made it wet. He look up at the television screen. Corinda had pulled Tim onto his back and was straddling his hips, the tip of his penis just parting her labia.

'This is like we were before,' Corinda said.

'Lick my balls,' Malcolm ordered.

The redhead rolled onto her back behind him, her head between his thighs, her mouth directly under his balls. She reached up and sucked them into her mouth. By the nature of her bondage her hands were held tight against his buttocks. She insinuated one finger to his anus and pushed it home.

'Good,' he said approvingly. 'Very good.'

'Come for me, darling,' Candy said, her own body pulsing with excitement, torn between watching the screen and watching her husband's cock.

'Come for me, Tim,' Corinda said. She sank down, forcing him deeper into her sex. Her right hand groped behind her back until her fingers fastened around his scrotum.

'Oh God,' Tim moaned.

Malcolm felt his spunk rising. The redhead was good. But then all the girls he bought from Constantine were good. He had no idea how he trained them or got them to cooperate so readily with their new masters, but his trips to Constantine's island were always a delight. It was not all pleasure, of course. It was business too.

Malcolm was a middle man. He paid Constantine a good price for all sorts of merchandise, to sell on at a profit, in London or Paris. But he made most from the girls. He had a client in Odessa, with a castle overlooking the Black Sea that had once belonged to Czar Nicholas I. He paid a great deal of money for the privilege of having first choice of the girls. What he didn't want he usually sent to Morocco at nothing like as healthy a mark-up. Fortunately the Russian wanted the two girls they had just picked up. They were on their way to deliver them now.

The redhead skewered her finger deeper into his anus and sucked harder on his balls, as he worked his hand up and down on his erection. He looked at the television, at Corinda riding Tim. He glanced down at his wife, the blonde's tongue buried in her pubic hair. Candy caught his eye.

'Spunk for me,' she said.

And he did. He was surrounded by sex, live and on the screen; too much provocation to hold out any longer. An arc of spunk shot out of his cock and splattered down onto the round cushions of his wife's tanned breasts.'

That was the last straw for her too. She closed her thighs, trapping the girl's face between them and ground her sex against her mouth, coming violently, her clitoris pulsing.

'Can you believe our luck?' Malcolm said when they had both recovered, watching eagerly as their new guests abandoned themselves to their own fevered orgasms.

Tim couldn't sleep. He lay on the bed with his eyes open. Something was wrong. He knew instinctively something was wrong. He lay on the bed staring out of the portholes at the stars, sparkling against the dark sky.

Corinda's breathing was regular. She was curled up on her side, naked. The night was too hot for even a single sheet. He could see she had fallen asleep with a smile on her face.

Something was wrong. He tried to concentrate on what it was. The Arlingtons had been perfectly charming. They had said and done nothing to alarm him in anyway, and yet he had this strange feeling of foreboding.

It wasn't until the first signs of light that he realised what it was. They were sailing into the sunrise, heading east, not west, not towards Gibraltar. They hadn't changed course all night so it couldn't just be a temporary heading to get around some obstacle. They were definitely not going to England.

Slipping out of bed he pulled on the borrowed shorts and T-shirt and stole silently out of the cabin, not wanting to disturb Corinda. He headed down the companionway. He had to find the Arlingtons. He was angry with them for lying. If they were going east he would demand they dropped them off at the nearest port.

He tried all the doors in the passage but they were locked. At the other side of the spiral stairs there was a wider corridor. At the far end there were double doors that looked as if they might be the master suite. Finding them unlocked he flung them open. The luxurious bedroom beyond was empty. Closing the doors he tried the one a little further back. Again it was open but the room was dark. He groped around until he found a light switch.

A metal hook was set into the ceiling in the centre of the small space. A chain hung down from it, the end of which was clipped to a D-ring at the front of the red leather collars around two girls' necks. Their hands were attached to the collars too. Apart from red leather corsets they were both naked. Gags had been stuffed into their mouths and strapped around their heads, their lips stretched around black rubber balls.

Tim recognised the girls immediately. From the window of his cell he had seen Eloisa escorting them into the beach house on three occasions. There was only one explanation as to why they were here now. The Arlingtons were in league with Constantine.

'Good morning.'

Tim spun round. Malcolm Arlington stood in the doorway. Two burly men stood behind him. 'An attractive picture, don't you think?'

'What are they doing here?' Tim said angrily.

'Get him out.'

The two men moved forward and pulled Tim out into the corridor. Malcolm slammed the door behind him.

'Like you, they think they are on their way to London, where they imagine I will free them. Like you they are going to be sadly disappointed.'

'You got them from Constantine.'

Candy appeared behind her husband's back. She was wearing a black one-piece swimsuit with a plunging neckline. 'Of course,' she said. 'And your bad luck has provided us with another prize.'

'We've been debating whether to keep her to ourselves or sell her on. We still can't decide,' Malcolm said.

'You, unfortunately,' Candy added, 'are surplus to requirements, however much I might fancy you.' She ran her hand over the front of Tim's shorts. 'Pity. Quite a weapon you've got there. Still, can't have everything.'

'Of course we realised you'd guess the truth when the sun came up. Which is why we don't allow them,' he gestured to the closed door, 'on deck, and why we've been waiting for you. The thing is, you are going to have to make a choice now, Mr Morrison. I can have my men throw you overboard; we're at least a hundred miles from land. Or I'll cut you adrift in your boat. Which would you prefer?'

'You bastard,' Tim said.

'Now if you would prefer the boat, then you are going to have to write a letter to your little friend. Just to say that you decided to go ashore to try and contact...'

'Arabella?' Candy suggested.

'Yes, that's right.'

'And what good will that do you?'

'Not a lot. It will buy us her cooperation for a while. She is very cooperative, isn't she? And we're both very much looking forward to *cooperating* with her. Aren't we, darling?'

'Mmm... very much.'

'If she notices we're heading east we'll tell her it's just a little detour to pick up a friend. Something like that. So I'm afraid you have to decide. What do you want to do, Mr Morrison?'

Chapter Eleven

'Good morning. I hope you slept well.'

Candy set the tray down on the bed. There was coffee and croissants, jam and butter, and a glass of freshly squeezed orange juice on a starched pink linen cloth.

Corinda woke slowly. The unexpected time change that had occurred when she'd escaped from the house had left her exhausted. For a moment she could not remember where she was. She looked around the cabin.

'Where's Tim?'

'Oh, he was up early. Apparently he's worried about Arabella. He decided, as we were passing a port, to put ashore to try and contact her. He said you'd understand. She'll obviously be worried sick. Here, he wrote you a note.'

Candy handed her a folded piece of paper. The note confirmed everything she had said.

'We've got a helicopter pad on deck. He's going to fly back when he's got through to her.'

'He's right. I've been worried about her too.' Corinda felt a wave of affection for him. He always thought of the right thing to do. It would be a terrific relief if Arabella knew they were safe. 'I'm starving.'

'No wonder; it's almost lunchtime. You've been asleep for hours. When you've finished we'll show you around the yacht.'

'That would be nice. You're really being so kind.'

'Not at all. It's our pleasure.'

Almost before Candy had closed the door behind her Corinda devoured the orange juice and a croissant. She spread jam thickly on a second, and then a third. Her adventures had left her ravenous.

She showered and washed her hair, then wrapped herself in one of the pink bath towels stacked in the bathroom, and found her way along the companionway and up the spiral staircase. The main stateroom led on to a large sundeck where Candy lay naked on her front on one of two white loungers.

'Hi,' she said. 'Feeling better?'

'Great,' Corinda said, staring at Candy's curvaceous bottom. She felt a wave of desire. It appeared her sexual impulses were never far from the surface. 'You're very beautiful.'

'Thank you. I try to keep in shape.'

'Do you like having sex with other women?'

Candy laughed. 'You are uninhibited, aren't you?'

'Shouldn't I say that?'

'Of course you should. Your openness is charming. And yes, I love having sex with women and men.'

Corinda sat on the other lounger. It was good to feel the sun on her body again. She slipped out of the towel without a second thought.

'Tim doesn't seem to think so,' she said.

'What?'

'About my openness. He finds it embarrassing.'

'He's very conventional. Some people can be very stuffy about sex. Malcolm and I are different.' Candy turned over onto her back, her breasts exposed to the sun.

'Stuffy?'

'Uncomfortable.'

'Why? I think it's just the best thing in the world. I mean, looking at you now. It makes me feel all squirmy inside.' She pressed her hand against her tummy. She found it hard to take her eyes off Candy's body. It reminded her of Arabella. 'Your breasts are so firm,' she said. 'I'd love to kiss them.'

'Feel free.'

Corinda slipped to her knees on the polished wooden deck and cupped Candy's right breast in her hand. She kissed the nipple lightly and felt it stiffen, her own doing exactly the same thing. She reached over and sucked the left nipple into her mouth. Her hand caressed Candy's belly, brushing against her pubic hair.

'Am I allowed to do this?' she asked.

'Of course. I told you, I love it.' Candy moved one leg until it was hanging over the edge of the lounger, her foot on the deck, leaving her sex exposed.

Corinda's finger worked its way between her labia. She found her clitoris. It pulsed as her finger touched it.

'Oh darling, that's lovely,' Candy said. 'Kiss me.'

Corinda pressed her lips to Candy's. She felt the woman's tongue dancing against her own.

'Well, that's a pretty picture.' Malcolm Arlington was standing in the stateroom doorway. 'Is this a private party or can anyone join in?' He was wearing a pair of yellow swimming trunks. His penis was already beginning to distend the tight material.

'She's got a lovely touch,' his wife said.

'I bet. Why don't I get the girls and we'll have a real party?'

'Good idea,' Candy agreed. Malcolm walked back inside.

'What girls?'

'You'll see. Don't stop.' Candy caught Corinda by the wrist and moved it up and down so her finger slid against her clitoris. 'Like that,' she said.

'You're very wet.'

'I know. You're very exciting.'

Corinda felt Candy tense. She kissed her breasts again, moving from one to the other, pinching both nipples with her teeth, each pinch cranking up the tension in Candy's body. Corinda saw her head arch back and the sinews of her throat stretch. She stroked her finger up and down. She had made Arabella come like this so many times and loved to watch it.

'Yes, darling, yes, that's perfect,' Candy muttered.

Her mouth opened wide and she shuddered, her body twitching twice in quick succession before the tension melted away. Immediately she closed her legs. 'No more,' she said.

'I'm so excited,' Corinda said, hoping Candy was going to reciprocate, as Arabella always had.

'Good. Come on. Let's go and see what Malcolm's organised for us.'

'Aren't we going to...?'

'Don't worry, darling, your turn will come.' That, she knew, was an understatement.

The small table was slightly lower than waist height. It had sturdy legs and its top was padded with suede. The two girls stood on either side of it. They were

121

still wearing their red corsets, but they also wore tight leather helmets that covered their heads entirely, apart from holes for their eyes and mouths. The helmet could not contain the redhead's hair, which was pulled through the lacing at the back to form a ponytail. They awaited instructions, eager to please the Arlingtons, prepared to do anything that would assure them safe passage away from Constantine.

Malcolm masked them in case Corinda had seen them on Constantine's island. She would find out the truth soon enough, but for the moment he wanted her acquiescence.

'Are you ready for us?' Candy asked, opening the door. The designer of the boat had intended the room as a gymnasium. The Arlingtons had converted it to their own purposes.

Corinda slipped inside and Candy closed the door. Malcolm was naked. A black leather strap was buckled tightly around the base of his erection and under his balls, and he'd had one of the girls apply oil to it so it shone under the lights. Candy kissed him, wriggling her naked body against him. The oil left a trail on her belly.

Corinda just stared at Malcolm's erection.

The girls had been told what to do. Candy sat on the edge of the table, then leant back. The surface was just large enough to accommodate her head and her torso, leaving her legs over the edge.

Corinda watched as the girls took Candy's wrists and buckled them into leather cuffs at the top corners of the table. Malcolm operated a small winch attached to a pulley over Candy's head. Hanging from the pulley by a rope was a metal bar with leather cuffs on each end. He lowered it until it was resting on Candy's chest and the rope was slack. The redhead took hold of it, pulled it all the way down to Candy's ankles, and fitted them one by one into the cuffs.

Malcolm operated the winch again, this time in the opposite direction. Corinda watched as Candy's legs were hauled upward, until her ankles were above her shoulders and her legs were pulled back at a forty-five degree angle to her torso. With her buttocks poised over the edge of the table, and her legs spread apart, her sex and anus were exposed.

'Well now, shall we begin?' Malcolm said.

The redhead stood in front of Candy's sex. She put her hands on either side of Candy's buttocks and leant forward, pushing her mouth against her sex and straightening her back, her legs apart. Candy moaned as the girl's tongue nudged against her sensitised clit.

Malcolm took the redhead by the hips and slid his cock into her. Corinda felt the excitement she had experienced on the sundeck coiling itself tighter within her body. Malcolm drove his cock deep into the girl's vagina.

'Does this excite you?' he asked Corinda.

'Yes,' she said breathlessly, her sex throbbing.

'Your turn then,' he said, pulling the redhead back. 'Do the same thing.'

Corinda moved into position quickly. She planted her mouth on Candy's sex and stuck her buttocks out just as the redhead had done. She pushed her tongue into Candy's vagina, and felt Malcolm's hands seizing her hips and his erection parting her labia. She wriggled her bottom against him and trapped his glans with her vagina.

Candy heard and felt the exclamation of pleasure Corinda made as she was penetrated. She loved the feeling of being bound and spread like this. She felt an orgasm beginning to grow, the first tingling sensations making her squirm. Corinda's tongue was wonderfully artful.

'My tits,' she hissed to the blonde. Immediately the girl's hands massaged and kneaded the firm flesh. She took hold of Candy's nipples and pulled her breasts up by them, stretching the flesh. 'Yes, yes,' Candy cried. They were supposed to use the blonde too, that was the plan; to have all three girls one after the other, each a human bridge between husband and wife. But Candy did not want to be parted from Corinda. Her mouth was too soft, her tongue too hot and too adept. Her orgasm was exploding. She strained against her bonds, her muscles taut, the constriction increasing her pleasure as it always did. Then the bubble of lust burst and she was flooded with a torrent of pleasure as her entire body spasmed.

Corinda thrust back on Malcolm's cock, Candy's climax provoking her own.

'Not yet,' he said pulling away, his cock slipping from her sex with a plop.

'Please,' she begged.

'I've got something more special in mind. Trust me,' he said.

The girls were unstrapping Candy's wrists and ankles. 'Very special,' she assured her.

'Here.' Malcolm went to a wooden frame like a single bed. It was covered with a thin mattress. 'Kneel up on here.'

Corinda was tingling. She knelt on all fours on the mattress. 'Like this?'

'Yes, just like that,' he said.

Candy got to her feet. She took a large vibrator from one of the storage units, and what looked like a tube of toothpaste.

'By the side of her,' she barked at the girls, who immediately knelt on the floor on either side of the frame.

'What are you going to do?' Corinda's voice was husky with excitement.

'Hush,' Candy said.

Malcolm knelt on the frame behind Corinda, his cock gleaming with her juices. She wriggled against it. She wanted to feel it driving into her again, filling her and opening her.

Candy knelt on the floor too. She unscrewed the cap of the tube and squeezed a colourless cream over her husband's erection. She rubbed more into the bud of Corinda's anus, then nudged the tip of the dildo against Corinda's clit.

'Have you used one of these before?'

'Yes,' Corinda replied. It moved and she felt it nose into her vagina. 'No,' she said, pouting. 'I want the real thing.' After the life of a real cock the dildo was a poor substitute.

'You're going to get it, don't worry,' Malcolm said, holding her hips firmly.

123

As Candy eased the dildo into her sex, Corinda felt the man's cock centre on her slippery, oiled anus. At first she thought it was the prelude to him working lower, but suddenly realised it was not. He was pushing.

'God... oh God,' she cried. A surge of excitement rushed through her so intensely she thought she might come. The dildo pushed deeper as the ring of muscles at her anus locked, then relaxed and his cock slid into her. She felt an extraordinary mixture of pain and pleasure. The cock paused, then pressed again and a second wave shot through her, except this time the pleasure was much stronger than the pain.

The two hooded girls each took one of her breasts. They squashed and mauled. The blonde used her other hand to find Corinda's clitoris. Every sexual centre was being attacked at once. The sensations coursing between them were unbelievable. As the cock pushed inward she came, her body shaking, her mind overwhelmed by the intensity of what she was feeling. But it didn't end there. As soon as she came down from the first high another was ready to take its place. She had never felt anything like it. Her vagina was contracting around the dildo, just as her anus seemed to be pumping on the erection. Malcolm was moving, provoking a whole new set of feelings. Two cocks inside her.

It seemed to go on and on. Candy moved the dildo in and out as the girls pinched her nipples. That pitched her to new heights. The blonde's finger stroked her clitoris, inducing another orgasm. Somewhere in the miasma of pleasure Corinda felt Malcolm's cock tense, swelling against the tight confines of her rear passage, the increased size making her gasp. She knew it meant he was going to come.

'Yes, do it,' she encouraged.

Candy jammed the dildo deep into Corinda's sex, as deep as it would go, and held it there. Malcolm pushed too, until his groin was hard against her buttocks and he was buried inside her completely. His cock jerked violently, then as his wife's hand jiggled against his balls it erupted spunk. His fingers dug into Corinda's hips as he closed his eyes and threw his head back. Instinct told him she had never been used like this before.

As she felt the cock convulsing her body seemed to clench around it. After the power and strength of the orgasms experienced in the last few minutes, she could not believe she was capable of coming again. But she was. An electric shock of raw pleasure coursed from her tortured nipples, down to her clitoris and arced from the head of the dildo to the head of his spunking cock, every nerve, every sinew, every taut muscle responding.

She came round slowly. It felt as though she had been knocked out. She was lying on the mattress, a sticky wetness leaking from between her legs. Candy, she saw, was standing by the door, unlacing the hood from one of the girls. In one corner, partially hidden behind a screen was a shower stall, and she could see the top of Malcolm's head as he showered.

Candy pulled the leather helmet from the redhead, who shook out her hair. She began on the blonde, pulling the laces from the little metal eyelets at the back. Slowly the tight leather loosened. With the laces freed she gripped the leather and pulled.

'No!' Malcolm snapped as he came around the screen and saw what his wife was doing.

It was too late. Candy had pulled the helmet off, and Corinda found herself staring into the face of the blonde who had entertained Eloisa and Yves so intimately.

'You stupid woman!' Malcolm cursed.

'What's she doing here?' Corinda sat up. She did not understand, the residue of extreme pleasure slowing her thought processes.

'What's the problem?' Candy asked.

'Why do you think I masked them? See?' He pointed at Corinda, whose expression had gone from puzzlement to realisation to alarm. 'She knows now!'

'I thought you'd just put the hoods on for fun,' Candy said.

'What's going on?' Corinda asked.

'Get them out of here,' Malcolm said. 'I'll deal with her.'

Candy marshalled the girls out of the door.

'You've been to the island, haven't you? Constantine's island,' Corinda demanded, realising there was a terrible implication in these developments. 'What have you done with Tim?'

Malcolm stood with his back to the door. 'Such a pity. I was looking forward to a repeat performance. Still, I must say the way we were going I'd have been very reluctant to part with you. Now I have no choice.'

'Where's Tim?' Corinda repeated.

'If you want the truth, I have absolutely no idea.'

She was very uncomfortable. They'd tied her hands and elbows together behind her back with nylon rope. Her ankles and knees were bound too, just as tightly, and she was lying on the mattress. Apart from being able to roll her body slightly she was completely powerless.

She was proud of the fact that she'd managed to scratch Malcolm's face and punch him in the eye before he overpowered her and, with the help of two of the crew, tied her up.

What he intended to do with her she didn't know, or care. The only thing she was concerned about was Tim. Clearly the Arlingtons were involved with Constantine in some way, which was probably why their yacht had been so close to the island. They might even take Corinda back to him, but however awful that prospect was she could only think about what they had done to Tim. Was he dead? Had they thrown him overboard? From the heights of ecstasy she had been plunged into the depths of despair.

She had no idea how long she had been tied up. Reminding her of the time on Constantine's island, the room had no windows and therefore no way to see the sun. It had been, she estimated, all day at the very least, and she was sure it was night outside now. The monotonous drone of the engines deep in the bowels and the gentle rolling of the yacht as it cut through the sea had remained unchanged.

She tried to sleep but her cramped muscles and numbed limbs made it difficult, even if she could manage to stop her mind racing through endless speculations. She found herself going over everything that had happened to her since she left Arabella. She had been so stupid. She should have seen through Constantine's lies from the start. Now the thought of him made her feel sick.

The fear that they were going to take her back to him dissipated. They would have arrived back on the island by now, if that was where they were heading. Her fate, she decided, did not lie with the Greek or the prince, who was no doubt fuming at the loss of his purchase.

The drone of the engines eventually lulled her to sleep, but she kept waking up. She thought of Tim and desperately wanted him to be safe, and tried to comfort herself with Malcolm's response to her question. If they'd killed him surely Malcolm wouldn't have said he didn't know where he was? But would they take the risk of casting him adrift in a boat? What if he were found and. managed to get to the authorities? Was the Mediterranean such a large sea that they didn't have to worry about that? All these thoughts swirled round in her head between bouts of fitful sleep.

She woke with a start, her heart thumping. The sound of an incessantly clanging bell filled the room, and she could hear feet running over the decks above her head. The noise of the engines changed to a different pitch and she felt the boat veer round sharply. Seconds later an explosion made the whole boat rock and Corinda could smell an acrid, diesel-laden aroma as smoke drifted under the door. Three or four much smaller explosions followed and the smoke intensified. Voices cried out in panic and alarm, while others were calmer, shouting orders.

More and more smoke curled under the door and began to fill the room. Corinda felt the boat judder to a halt and the engine noise died.

The pandemonium above continued. She heard feet running in all directions, and a dull clunk as if something had hit the hull. It was probably the lifeboat being lowered, she thought, with the Arlingtons safely aboard.

Suddenly the handle on the door twisted. The door was locked and whoever was outside did not have a key. They had come prepared for that; a sledgehammer smashed through the lock and the door was thrown open. A muscular man dressed entirely in black, with a black ski-mask over his face, stood in the open doorway. Dropping the hammer he picked Corinda up as easily as if she were a sack of feathers, and hoisted her over his shoulder.

Within seconds they were out in the corridor. Another man in the same outfit was waiting for them. The corridor was full of smoke, but they found their way up the spiral staircase and out into the main stateroom. Corinda strained to see what was happening. It was night and a fire lit up the bow of the ship, smoke billowing from it in a black cloud. Members of the crew were trying to fight the blaze.

The two men ran to the stern. They threw a blanket over her, and still carrying her on his shoulder, and apparently without effort, the man climbed down into a waiting motorboat. His companion followed, cast off and gunned the engines. The boat surged away from the yacht and sped out across the sea.

Corinda looked up. There, silhouetted against a horizon lit by a moon that was now full, was another much smaller yacht. She knew immediately what had happened. Constantine had come after her. This was his boat and his men. He'd worked out that the Arlingtons had been nearby and were the most likely to pick her up, and had somehow tracked their yacht. She was being taken back to his island and to the prince.

The motors throttled back and the boat bumped against the side of its parent yacht. Corinda, still bound in a tight bundle, was picked up bodily again, pitched over the man's shoulder and carried up to the deck. The man walked into the main cabin and lowered her gently onto a sofa. The blanket had flipped over her face, making it impossible for her to see.

'Get a knife.' It was a woman's voice. She recognised it immediately. She recognised her perfume too.

A hand pulled the blanket away from her body, and Corinda gazed up into a smiling face.

'Arabella! Oh, Arabella! How on earth did you find me? It's so good to see you. I've missed you. How did you manage to find the yacht? I can't believe it.' The words came tumbling out.

The man in the mask began to slice through the rope bonds with a hunting knife.

'Are you all right? Are you hurt?'

Freed from the ropes Corinda began rubbing her wrists and ankles. 'I think I'm fine,' she said.

'Nikos, get a robe and some brandy, will you?' The man pulled off his ski-mask and headed for an inner door.

'How did you find me?'

'It's a long story.'

'And Tim. What about Tim?'

'He's safe.'

'Really? Really? Where is he?'

The man in black returned with a white towelling robe, a bottle of brandy and two glasses.

'Thank you, Nikos.'

The man retreated, a little reluctantly, as Corinda's voluptuous body disappeared under the robe.

Arabella poured the brandy. 'He's gone to get the authorities, so they can rescue the other two girls. He'll be back by morning. That yacht's not going anywhere. The men made sure they crippled the engines.'

'I can't believe you found me.'

Arabella sat next to her. 'We picked up a distress signal from the yacht the night you left. I hired this boat and scoured the area. It was completely clean. But the captain said he'd heard about lots of boats being lost in a channel to the west, so we went there and found wreckage. I landed on the island. There was a strange white Greek with pink eyes. He said he hadn't seen anything.'

'You met Constantine? You were in the house?' Corinda was astonished. Arabella had been so close.

'Yes. I didn't trust him. I kept circling the island. Eventually I saw that yacht.' She pointed across the water. The flames were out now, but a plume of smoke still rose into the moonlit sky. 'I saw them take two girls aboard. That made me even more suspicious, so I tried to follow them. We must have been too far away to see you taken aboard. It was dark. But then, last night, we saw them cast the motorboat adrift. We picked it up and found Tim. So we planned the fire as a diversion to get you out.'

'Oh that's wonderful, Arabella!' Corinda wrapped her arms around her tutor and hugged her tightly.

'I think you should get some sleep now. You must be exhausted.'

'No, Arabella. I don't want to sleep. I want you. I want to feel you again. Take me to bed. That's what I really want.'

And it was true. Her sexual excitement at seeing and touching dear Arabella again was intense. The pulse of desire and lust she felt for her was as sharp as it had ever been. She kissed her, as her hand pushed down into Arabella's lap, feeling again the familiar contours of her body.

Hyde Park was in full flower, the grass at its greenest, the ornamental borders a riot of colourful blossoms. The sun was setting and a salmon-pink sky, mottled with high cirrus cloud, provided a backdrop for the trees, the light filtering through their branches. Corinda gazed out of the hotel window at the spectacle. Her room was on the seventh floor and she had a panoramic view. The park and the teeming city all around it, the cars and bustle of Park Lane, were like nothing she'd seen before.

She had ordered a bottle of champagne from room service. The knock on the door of the suite indicated it had arrived. She opened it to a young waiter in a white linen jacket.

'Come in,' she said.

His mouth gaped and he started to blush.

'Oh, sorry.' Corinda realised the reason for his embarrassment. She was naked. She still found it hard to remember to get dressed, and to understand the effect her naked body had on men. She closed the door rapidly, grabbed a pink satin robe and wrapped it around her body, before opening the door again. 'I'm so sorry,' she said to the startled waiter. 'I just forgot.'

The young man shuffled in, put the tray on the nearest table and almost ran out again without a word. The image of her naked body, her full breasts, her flat stomach and the downy pubic hair at its base, was going to stay with him for a long time.

Corinda looked at her watch. It was time to get ready. The yacht had put into port and Arabella had insisted Corinda fly to London, out of harm's way, while Tim sorted out everything with the Greek authorities. That was three days ago. She had decided to stay in a hotel. She didn't want to go to her father's house until Tim returned. She didn't want to be on her own.

She hadn't spent any time with him since their night together on the Arlington's yacht, but tonight, at last, everything had been taken care of in Athens and he was flying in. His plane would have landed already and he had promised her on the telephone that he would come straight to the hotel.

The clothes she'd bought on her first shopping expedition were laid out on the bed. She had bought them all with this moment in mind. Walking through to the bedroom she stripped off the satin robe and sat on the bed. There was a cellophane packet of stockings. She opened it and shook the nylon out. As she rolled the first stocking into a pocket and fitted it over her toes, she could not help but remember the first time she had done exactly the same thing, in her strange windowless cell with Eloisa. The thought made her go cold. She dismissed it from her mind and concentrated on what she was doing, watching the way the sheer black nylon encased her leg. She eased the black welt up to her thigh, then repeated the process with the second stocking.

She had bought a black satin basque, with a lace inset at the front. As she wrapped it around her body and fastened the hooks that held it tightly in place, she experienced again that odd thrill the constriction seemed to create. The bra cups were made from lace. Her breasts swelled out from them, her nipples barely covered. She clipped the suspenders, ruched in black satin, into the welts of the stockings and adjusted them so the nylon was held taut, then slipped her feet into black leather shoes with high heels.

There was a wall of wardrobes in the bedroom, with mirrored doors. She examined herself critically. She liked the way the heels shaped and firmed the muscles of her legs and enhanced the curve of her bottom. The basque left her buttocks uncovered, their flesh smooth and creamy, asking to be pampered and caressed.

That's what she wanted. She wanted to feel Tim holding her again. She wanted to feel his muscles pressing against her softness, his erection growing against her tummy. A thrill of pleasure coursed through her. She looked in the mirror and watched her hand slide down the lace panel at the front of the basque, over its delicately scalloped hem, to the downy fur of her pubis. Her finger delved between her labia and found her clitoris. She stroked it gently, building upon the initial moment of excitement. She angled her finger and was not surprised by the wetness she found. Despite her efforts to exclude them her mind was full of memories, and they were at least partially responsible for her condition. However much she tried to hate them, she could not forget the extremes of pleasure she had experienced with Constantine, Eloisa, Yves and the prince. Just the thought of what they had done to her, how thoroughly they had exploited her body, produced a fluttering in the pit of her stomach which spread rapidly to her sex, making it slick with her juices.

And that was to say nothing of the Arlingtons. Malcolm had completed her sexual education, and taken away the last vestige of innocence. It was another profound and unforgettable experience, another pleasure she wanted to repeat.

She had no idea what life would hold for her from now on, but she knew what she wanted and the time she had spent on Constantine's island taught her exactly how to get it. She knew what affect her body had on men, and she had learnt how to use it.

There was knock at the door. Tim. At last. She rushed into the sitting room. He wouldn't be able to resist her; no man would. She knew that now. In seconds she would feel that hard cock thrusting into the silky wet depths of her sex.

'Tim,' she said, opening the door.

'Corinda.' He looked at her, his eyes roaming over her body. 'You look... you look... jeez, Corinda. How am I supposed to resist you?'

'You're not,' she said emphatically.

The Slaves of New York, also published by us and available as a paperback at AMAZON

A man had silently entered the room. Because of the position of her head she could not see much of his body, but his face was tanned.

Kim remembered she had to kneel. Without the use of her arms it was a difficult manoeuvre, but she managed it.

The man moved closer. Now she could see him properly. He was naked and his body was lean, completely free of hair except for a thick bush at his groin. His cock was flaccid and uncircumcised.

'My name is Cantrell,' he said. 'You must call me, sir. Do you understand?'

'Yes, sir,' Kim said at once...

Fascinated by the erotic masterpieces of the reclusive Jake Ashley, beautiful young journalist Kate Holbrook determines to interview him. She goes to New York, where she discovers a living reality just as bizarre as anything in Ashley's books; men and women prepared to become slaves and do anything for their masters. And it appears that the only way to meet Ashley in person is to become one of them.

Kate soon attracts Jake's attentions and is taken to his secluded house. He proves to be a strict and demanding master, and with her new found penchant for bondage and submission Kate is taken to new heights of passion. But she discovers that some major celebrities visit the house, their involvement there the kind of story that could seriously advance her career. Will she try to escape and get her story published, or will she remain a **Slave of New York**?